UNGUARDED LOVE

DANIEL & NITA

KALYN COOPER

Unguarded Love

KaLyn Cooper

Cover Artist: Drue Hoffman

Editor: Marci Boudreaux Clark, Rebecca Hodgkins

Spanish Translator: Cymbeline Nunez

Published 2018, 2020

ISBN: 978-1-970145-14-4

ISBN: 978-1-970145-22-9 – Spanish Translation

A LETTER TO READERS

Dear Reader,

Welcome to novel #4 of the Black Swan series.

Unguarded Love is a stand-alone contemporary romance novel that picks up the Black Swan story at the end of the novella *Challenging Love* but it can be read by itself.

After a tragedy in med school, Nita Banks decided she never wanted anything to do with treating sick children ever again. When Ebola breaks out in the middle of a Central American coup, she has her hands full between missions and helping the CDC find a cure.

As an undercover CIA agent, Daniel Callahan was an expert at keeping secrets. None of his family or American friends knew about his two children until his baby daughter became sick, and adults were dying all around him. The only person he trusted with her care was his first true female friend, Nita. Even though she's his sister's good friend and teammate, the feelings he has for her are far from familial.

When Nita discovers Daniel's baggage includes a diaper bag and a rollie with superheroes on it, she'll have to face her fears or lose both the baby and Daniel.

Thank you for purchasing *Unguarded Love.* If you enjoy this book, consider purchasing the other books in the **Black Swan series** as well as the related **Guardian Elite series**

All books are listed on www.KaLynCooper.com with links to all formats.

Always,
   KaLyn Cooper

DEDICATION

I dedicate this book to active-duty women who serve on medical staffs in combat.

ACKNOWLEDGMENTS

For every book I write, there are so many people who help me along the way. I'd like to send a special thanks to all the members of the Black Swan Book Club. You guys help me in more ways than you'll ever know. Your opinions and suggestions often guide and inspire me. Many thanks to Debbie Workman and Tracey Moore Presley who named characters in this book. My deepest thanks to my physician, Dr. Nancy Bartley, who tolerates my unusual medical questions and helps keep some of those aspects of my books relatively accurate, but I often take literary license. And to William Russell, who was in medical school rotations shadowing her and suggested Reston Ebola. It was the perfect virus. I'd like to thank my "Lunch Bunch", especially romantic suspense author Rachel Rivers who shared her first-hand cop experience with me so a vital scene could be as realistic as possible. Author Vikki Vaught, I can't thank you enough for your beta reading, insight and encouragement. Marci Clark has my deepest gratitude for the magic she works on my words and the whip she cracks to keep me writing on schedule so I can continuously bring new stories to my readers. Drue Hoffman, thanks for another great cover and awesome publicity. Last, thank you to my husband for your continual support.

ABOUT THE BLACK SWAN SERIES

Rara avis in terris
is Latin for
"a rare bird in the lands."

In the ancient world, it was believed that the landing of a single black swan created a change that would affect the entire world. In today's world, that change can be seen almost instantly…9/11 is the best example.

Fact: Nicaragua is looking to build a new canal between the Caribbean Sea/Atlantic Ocean and the Pacific Ocean that is wider than the aging Panama Canal. Many ships today are too large for the narrow Panamanian passage.

Fact: Reston Ebola is real, and named for Reston, Virginia where dozens of monkeys died from Ebola. It was one of the first cases where Ebola was transmitted from monkeys to humans and traveled airborne.

Fact: Men always underestimate beautiful women.

CHAPTER 1

"Fifty yards to go," Lady Harrier reassured the hobbling Marine she supported on her left side. She stared through the sights on her M4 rifle snugged against her right shoulder, finger on the trigger. The door that would lead them both to freedom was within sight. "You can do this." The words were a promise to herself as much as to the injured man.

"Lady Hawk clear with three female packages. No major injuries." Thank goodness her team leader had rescued the imprisoned women. They were in better shape than expected. Good. That would make her triage easier and extrication faster.

"Lady Eagle exiting the south side. Need a medic. GSW shoulder, side and foot." Their team's primary pilot and second sniper had her hands full. That poor soldier had several gunshot wounds.

"I need medics. Lady Falcon's been shot," Lady Kite stated coolly between heavy breaths.

Oh, fuck. Lady Harrier's friend had been shot. The fist that grabbed her heart released the next second.

This is only a drill. It's only a drill. She repeated the mantra with every labored step. This damn Marine was heavy.

"Coming out south side, now," Lady Kite announced. "I hope to Christ you have those medics waiting because Lady Falcon is bleeding all over me and there are two Marines right behind me. One has an ankle injury and the other was shot in the thigh."

No. This is not real. Lady Falcon is not shot. She is not bleeding all over Lady Kite. This is only a drill. We are practicing.

Lady Harrier had to get her mind off the words bouncing between her heart and her head. She needed to think of something else.

Daniel Callahan's face inches away before he closed the distance and laid his lips on hers. That was definitely a distracting image. The kiss he'd given her just before she'd left Costa Rica a month ago shouldn't keep invading her mind. But it did. This time the memory proved the welcome diversion she needed.

Something skittered in her peripheral vision. Looking through the infrared scope, she watched a large rat duck into the open door a few feet ahead on her right. That room had been cleared earlier, and all the rodent would find was empty darkness. She glanced around, but saw nothing unusual.

"Look, we're halfway to the door." She was supposed to be reassuring her patient, not thinking about the night she and Daniel had spent together...talking. Just talking.

She'd spent lots of nights with men, but they seldom talked. She had always preferred action to words. Their mouths had better things to do than spew lies and platitudes she didn't need to hear to reach an orgasm. She needed the man's mouth licking and sucking.

Sudden weight on her left side and a heavy grunt brought her out of her fantasy of Daniel's head between her legs. "We're almost there. You can make it. Only a few more steps."

"Eighteen minutes, forty-six seconds. Not bad, ladies, but not good enough," the gunnery sergeant in charge of the training exercise yelled in a deep voice as Lady Harrier threw open the door and stepped into the Virginia sunshine with her supposedly injured Marine.

He immediately stood. "You're stronger than you look for such a little bit." His Texas drawl was nearly as charming as his smile. Full lips surrounded two rows of straight white teeth. She imagined those soft lips kissing her everywhere. His brown eyes twinkled in the bright Quantico sun as though he shared her thoughts.

He was cute. Definitely fuckable. And fuck, she needed a man.

His gaze dropped to her chest which showed off her perky breasts even through the black T-shirt and night camouflage uniform. He stood straighter and lost the smile as he added, "Ma'am."

She took in six feet of all-man in Marine Dress Blues—broad shoulders, and, yep, there were red stripes on his bicep. Enlisted. Off limits. Erasing any intensions she had about exploring his muscle structure under that black jacket, she nodded. "Sergeant. I might be height-challenged, but I'm innovative. Be glad I didn't decide to drag your sorry ass down that hallway on a carpet. If you had any other injuries and couldn't walk with my limited assistance that was my next option."

"Yes, ma'am." He glanced over his shoulder at the other Embassy School students participating in the training. "Permission to be excused, Captain."

Sometimes Lady Hawk forgot her Army rank. Hell, she and the other Ladies of Black Swan wore civilian clothes so much, she often forgot she was still in the military. They spent most of their time at Homeland Security, and on missions where no one wore their rank. It took her by surprise as she looked down at her chest and saw two black bars embroidered between buttons. Her eyes met his. "Granted."

She watched the very fine specimen of American Marine as he strode toward the other men gathered twenty yards away.

"Too bad." Lady Falcon stepped up next to Lady Harrier.

"Yeah, it's a real bitch that we have to do this again." She never took her eyes off the nearly perfect ass on the Marine. Matter of fact, every one of them looked nearly perfect. All were at least six feet tall, broad shouldered, and with a trim waist accented by the white belt on the dress blues. Each was good-looking with a hard edge about him, but that was to be expected. Marines couldn't even apply for Embassy Guard duty unless they'd had at least one combat tour. Most of those men had spent a year or more in the desert toting a gun and a heavy backpack.

"That too," Lady Falcon admitted. "I was talking about our training-induced dry spell. I swear most of the men on Marine Corps Base Quantico are either fresh out of college over at TBS, or they've been married for years and are attending the Command and Staff College."

"I wonder where all the FBI recruits hang out at night?" Lady Harrier turned toward her friend and teammate. "You have to be at least twenty-six to even apply to the FBI. That puts them within a few years of us. Not that I'm averse to dating younger men. Most of them take direction well."

"I'd just like to date something other than Bob, at least for one night." Lady Falcon was referring to her battery-operated boyfriend.

"I know exactly what you mean." Although Lady Harrier had named her favorite toy Channing, it wasn't the same as having a man between her legs. Daniel immediately popped into her mind. She wondered just how talented he would be with his mouth, his fingers, and his cock.

"Sorry, ladies." Lady Hawk stepped next to Lady Falcon. "They're keeping us on a short leash for a reason. I expect we'll be called out within twenty-four hours."

Lady Harrier glanced over her shoulder at the training village where they had run through various scenarios for nearly forty-eight hours, both day and night. Each member of her team had been tested, and the situation had been analyzed and dissected. They were as ready as they were ever going to be.

Or so they thought.

～

Forty hours later, Lady Harrier pulled off bloody surgical gloves and sealed them in a Ziploc bag. "Were going to get you out of here right away." She held the bare ankle of a Marine sergeant who was about five years younger than her. He probably thought it was for comfort, but she was counting his pulse and reassuring herself that blood was reaching his foot.

"No, ma'am," he protested. "We have to get all the embassy personnel out first."

The ambassador and the minister had already been airlifted along with a dozen or so members of the diplomatic corps. Most had sent their families home weeks ago when rumblings of a coup in the African nation had reached a level of concern. Constant updates came through the communication system in her ear, and she couldn't miss the thumping of large helicopters landing on the roof.

Active gunfire outside the brick and block walls reassured her the SEAL team sent in with them as protection was doing its job. The man on the table was a member of the embassy's security team. His injury was the most serious she'd seen since infiltrating. He needed to be on the next flight out, and then immediately taken to Germany where they could operate on his leg.

"Actually, sergeant, that's not your decision to make." Lady Harrier didn't take shit from anybody. He'd been shot in his muscular thigh. She was pretty sure the bullet had nicked his femur, but without an x-ray, there was no way she could tell for sure. The tablet-sized x-ray she was testing just wasn't clear enough for an accurate assessment. He'd been bleeding so badly, Lady Falcon had called for her assistance as soon as she'd found him. Good thing, too. If he had bled out much longer, he was going to need more than the platelet transfusion she'd already given him.

Thanks to the clotting agents she carried in her medical pack, she was able to stop the bleeding. That was the good news. The bad news was the extraction point had been changed to the roof, and they had to get all two hundred twenty pounds of muscled Marine with an attitude up four flights of stairs.

"Lady Harrier, this is Lady Hawk. I need you to trade places with me, right now."

Lady Hawk and Lady Eagle had been responsible for retrieving the three women remaining in the embassy. If Lady Harrier was needed, that meant there was a major problem.

"We need to get this patient to the roof and out of here immediately." Lady Harrier glanced toward Lady Falcon who stood guard at the door. Her nod indicated the hallway was clear.

"Lady Harrier, I'll take care of that. Your expertise is needed here." Their team leader sounded as though she was on the move.

"Lady Hawk, this is Lady Harrier. Moving your way with one injured." She could carry the man if she had to, but he had one good leg. She wiggled herself under the arm on his good side and let her much taller friend, Lady Falcon, support him on the injured side.

They had just turned the second corner toward the stairs when Lady Hawk opened the stairwell door. "I've got him. The women were not in their assigned quarters. We found them in the infirmary. We've already taken two of them to the roof, but I don't know if we can move the third one yet or not. Only you can make that decision." Lady Hawk seamlessly slid under the Marine's arm, freeing Lady Harrier to dash up the steps.

Because they had practiced so much in Quantico, she knew exactly where the infirmary was located.

What she found upon arrival was the last thing she ever expected to encounter in an embassy under siege.

Lady Harrier estimated the young woman's age to be mid-twenties. Her red face and exhausted eyes told the first half of the story. Her feet propped in stirrups spread wide, explained Lady Hawk's comment.

The woman was having a baby.

Baby. Baby. The word echoed in her mind as the edges of her vision darkened and closed in. Nita couldn't breathe.

She stared at the white sheet draped over long suspended legs and knew what was underneath.

Lady Harrier started to turn around to leave. She had to get the fuck out of there. Right. Now.

She didn't do babies.

Not since medical school rotations. Not since her lifelong plans to become a military physician were shattered in one shallow breath followed by a long exhale.

"Good, Lady Harrier is here. She'll take good care of you and your baby." Lady Eagle's statement froze Nita in place.

She gasped in air. Not enough to clear her tunnel vision, but enough to circulate oxygen around her body and keep her on her feet.

Her stomach clenched in fear, an emotion she hadn't felt in years. She'd been in firefights plenty of times and had never been this afraid. She'd been stripped naked and beaten during a mission in Iraq and hadn't been this scared.

She looked at her shaking hands and wondered if her feet would move so she could run away.

Get your shit together, Nita. Her mental chastisement helped...a little.

She had a moral and legal obligation to take care of this woman...and the child inside her.

She had the training and had actually delivered over one hundred babies while still in med school. But the unborn child inside the woman on the hospital bed frightened her to the point she could not move.

Whump. Whump. Whump. The landing of the next helicopter shook the building. Lady Harrier hoped her teammates had gotten the young sergeant to the roof for evacuation.

With that momentary distraction, she sucked in a much-needed breath.

Lady Eagle stared at her. With her fingers hidden from the couple in the room, she used their own unique sign language to ask if Lady Harrier was okay. Was she hurt?

No. Not hurt. Just immobile. She signed back

Physiologically, Lady Harrier could move. Psychologically, she couldn't force her brain to make her feet step in front of the other.

The woman on the bed moaned and rubbed her large abdomen. She pinched her face as she attempted breathing techniques taught during childbirth classes.

"Oh, thank God you're here, doctor." The man wasn't much taller than Nita, maybe five feet ten inches, but his grip was strong as he shook her hand. "I'm Ken Walker, the charge d'affaires, and this is my wife Diana. She's the protocol officer here." He gave Nita a half smile. "At least we were."

He pulled, and Lady Harrier had no excuse but to follow him back to the side of the bed.

"She's pregnant," he added as though it wasn't obvious.

"No shit, Sherlock," Lady Harrier sniped before she could hold her tongue in check. Hoping they both let it slip, she asked the next routine question. "How far along is she?"

"Thirty-eight weeks and two days," Diana quickly answered.

Whew. Nearly to term. The last thing Lady Harrier wanted was to deliver a premature baby.

She placed her hand on top of Diana's distended belly. Gently feeling for the position of the baby, which seemed to be head down and in position. God was looking favorably on her today. She wasn't sure if she could perform a cesarean section with the limited surgical implements she carried in her medical kit. "Has her water broken?"

"No, not like they showed us in the movie in the birthing class." Ken took his wife's hand and kissed the back of her knuckles. "You're doing great, sweetheart."

Lady Eagle interrupted, "It looks like you've got this. I'm going to clear this floor." She disappeared down the hall.

Got this? Not really. Lady Harrier hadn't had anything to do with a baby in years. That was by her choice. She wasn't at all comfortable with babies. She'd rather face an armed terrorist than a tiny newborn human.

Lady Harrier moved along with the expected questions. "How often are the contractions?"

"They kind of come and go." Diana spoke calmly and looked at her husband for confirmation.

Well, at least the woman isn't hysterical and screaming. Lady Harrier knew just how tough women were. She'd treated enough emergency cases of gunshots, knife wounds, broken bones, and damaged soft tissue from beatings that she was well aware of the pain levels that women could endure, practically without complaint. The woman in front of her wasn't in any real pain.

"They were coming about every fifteen minutes," Ken noted, "but then they just stopped."

Thank fuck! Maybe I won't have to do anything after all. Knowing what came next, Lady Harrier warned Diana, "I need to check you and see how far you're dilated." Quickly snapping on gloves, she moved down to the end of the table and sat on the rolling stool. "You'll feel a little pressure as I insert my fingers into your vagina canal." She was only dilated two centimeters and the cervical plug was still in place. With one hand on top of the bulge, she pressed gently on the baby to see if perhaps Diana was further along the process. Almost no movement in the cervix.

Lady Harrier let out a long, slow breath. She closed her eyes. *Thank you God and baby Jesus.*

Gunfire coming from the floor beneath them brought her out of her prayer. Through her earpiece she heard a report that the embassy Marines were clearing floor by floor, double-checking to be sure no one had been left behind.

She stood and stripped the gloves off her hands. Removing her communication unit from her ear, she replaced it with the stethoscope. She smiled at the nervous couple, then announced, "I'm pretty sure you're not in labor. I'm going to listen to your baby's heartbeat just to be sure it's not under stress."

She blocked out everything except for the rapid thumping in her ears, glanced at the large watch on her wrist, and began counting heartbeats. She wondered if they knew they were having a boy. She yelped in surprise when the unborn infant kicked at her hand.

She lifted the stethoscope and shoved it back in her pack. Catching herself before she used the pronoun *he,* she announced, "Your baby has a healthy heart beat and isn't ready to come out quite yet."

"What about the contractions?" Concern was evident in the father's voice.

Lady Harrier screwed the tiny comm unit back into her ear. "You need to get dressed immediately. We have to get you out of here."

If they could get her on the transport sitting on the roof, she could make it to civilization before having her baby.

"Operations control, this is Lady Harrier. I have two and a half that need to be on the next flight out before this baby decides it wants to be born in Africa."

CHAPTER 2

DANIEL CALLAHAN EMERGED ONTO THE CRESCENT BEACH then looked over his shoulder for the umpteenth time since leaving the tent encampment in Nicaragua. He'd crossed into Costa Rica a few miles back and instantly felt safer, even though few people paid attention to the lines drawn on paper maps.

As he stepped onto the familiar white sand, calm washed over his body. He was home. Well, almost. The sand he walked upon was owned by his sister, Katlin, and their uncle Monsignor Francis Gilpatrick. Daniel, and their only other living relative, Uncle Tom, owned the property on the opposite side of the Callahan compound including the upscale resort hotel. But that was not his destination tonight.

No, he and Uncle Tom would meet in the family owned, very private house that was once a small hotel, similar to an American-style bed-and-breakfast. Tonight's meeting would not be a family reunion. He'd been summoned for a serious discussion.

His beloved uncle Tom Gilpatrick was also the deputy director of the CIA, Daniel's boss, and his surrogate father since he turned twelve. His own father had been too busy gallivanting the world from embassy to embassy, climbing the military ladder all the way to the rank of Marine Corps Major General, to worry about the son he'd left behind in the United States. But his parents had taken Daniel's precious little sister, Katlin, with them each and every move. Meanwhile, he had been left in the care of his paternal grandparents and the staff of the military school.

Daniel didn't have time to think about that pain in his heart. It was buried six feet deep, along with his father. Fortunately, being undercover in Nicaragua had been the perfect excuse why he hadn't attended his father's funeral four years ago.

But the man who had filled that gap in his life was waiting for him up ahead. Daniel ducked under a long palm tree that extended nearly to the lapping Caribbean Sea. Using the tree as cover, he stood watching the moonlit beach for any motion, searching for any shadow that didn't belong. The hairs on the back of his neck had tingled since he'd left his so-called cohorts stumbling drunk and chasing the many available women in camp.

Leaving that night had been nearly impossible. His instructions had been to tell no one of this clandestine meeting, not even his best friend, Santiago. He hoped Uncle Tom had given Rosita the night off so she wouldn't ask about her son.

Daniel slid soundlessly through a side door and was met by a gun to the head followed by a sigh of relief.

"Next time, text me and let me know it's you." The man in his mid-fifties took a deep breath and holstered his gun.

"I love you, too, Uncle Tom." Daniel took his hand off the

gun strapped to his thigh. "Now, why the fuck am I here?" He flicked off the light and peered through one of the side windows, tracing his path back to the tree.

"Were you followed?" Concern wove through the older man's words.

"I don't think so." Daniel continued staring at the tree line. "I just have a gut feeling that the back of my head is in somebody's crosshairs."

"Most likely it's those fucking monkeys again." Tom walked toward the wet bar in one corner of the large living room. He poured two fingers of eighteen-year-old scotch into heavily leaded crystal glasses. Picking up one, he headed toward the living room. They had done this often enough that Daniel knew the other glass was for him.

Tonight, he needed it.

By the time Daniel stepped into the seating area, his uncle had already made himself comfortable in an overstuffed chair. "What's so fucking important that you called me here with zero notice?"

As Daniel settled into the couch, he realized it was the same seat he had taken the night he had spent with Nita. Memories washed over him like sinking into a bubbling spa tub. Heat rushed through his body from his toes to his shoulders, light touches bringing every nerve ending in his skin to life. Seldom had he ever spent the night with a woman with all his clothes on. Yet, he had so enjoyed her intelligent conversation, snarky banter, and wit.

"I'm sure you're aware that the political structure in Washington has changed, again." Uncle Tom's words brought Daniel out of the recollections of one of the best nights he'd had in years.

Daniel didn't miss a beat. "I might live in a Third World shit hole, but everyone pays attention to the United States."

"What you might not know is that along with that political change, there's been a dramatic swing in opinions toward the Nicaraguan government."

As his favorite uncle sipped the dark brown alcohol, Daniel noticed the pronounced worry lines across his forehead. The overhead recessed lighting seemed to reflect off more gray hair. Tom was two years younger than Daniel's mother would have been had she not been killed in a car accident nearly six years earlier. He wondered if her naturally blond hair would have grayed, or simply turned a beautiful platinum. Katlin looked so much like her. She even had their mother's outgoing personality, but his little sister had developed the same drive to succeed as their father.

Daniel shook his head as though to clear it. This was a business meeting. He shouldn't be thinking about family. Perhaps it was just being inside the house he and his sister owned—the place they had inherited from their parents—that brought back the longing for family. Every holiday, and several weeks during the summer, he would join Katlin and their parents in this house. They would be a complete family, for a while. All too soon he'd have to return to the United States, back into the guardianship of his grandparents and the strict rules of the military school he hated. Daniel would never put his children through that kind of life. No matter what, he would take his children with him. Although, right now, that was a moot point.

"Son, are you all right?" Uncle Tom leaned forward with his elbows on his knees and a nearly empty glass in his clasped hands.

No. He wasn't all right...and probably never would be. "Just a little tired." It was the truth. "I'm sorry, sir, you were telling me about the change that came with the last election."

"The new president of the United States doesn't really

care for his Nicaraguan counterpart." Tom stared at the empty glass before getting up to refill it. "It seems the two men had a business run-in long before our new president had political aspirations. The Nicaraguan president didn't like the idea of an American businessman mining gold, silver, and copper from *his* mountains." Uncle Tom grinned. "But he didn't mind taking all those American dollars to allow the geologic surveys."

"No, I wasn't aware there was any connection between the two presidents, but it doesn't surprise me. The Nicaraguan president isn't known for playing nice." Daniel thought for a moment then asked the million-dollar question. "So, what are you saying? Is the United States going to back a coup?"

"There is a reason that you have been deep undercover for so many years." Tom finished pouring another glass of scotch and returned the bottle to the well-stocked bar. "Let's just say your boss, Cristobal Maximo, is about to become a very rich man, not to mention popular. We will be increasing our arms shipments through you, and thus him."

The look his uncle gave Daniel was all too familiar. There was more. And it wasn't good.

"General DeLeon Cortez is going to want to meet with your boss. Make sure that happens." That was a direct order and both men knew it.

"Is Cortez going to be willing to make a deal that Cris is going to want?" Daniel sure as hell hoped so.

"Ever since our election, we've had some of our best special operators training General Cortez's men in Honduras." His uncle never raised his eyes from the ice tinkling in his glass.

Why the fuck hadn't Daniel been told about this?

Before he could ask the question, Uncle Tom admitted, "It was need to know only and USSOCOM is only a half-step away from paranoia these days. General Lyon knows he has a mole."

Daniel connected the dots within minutes. "Is Katlin and her team in Honduras now?" Women had often played important roles in military coups around the world.

Tom's gaze met his, but the man said nothing. His silence was confirmation. The idea that his sister and her team, which included Nita, were only a few hundred miles away, excited Daniel. He might get the opportunity to spend more time with the brilliant woman with soft brown curls that framed her girl-next-door face.

He really had to focus on the problem at hand.

"So, the United States is going to kick out a standing president because of a business deal gone bad, five or ten years ago?" Daniel tried to wrap his head around the political reasons, not that it was really important. Like any other good government employee, he did what he was told and kept his mouth shut.

"Fuck, no," Tom shot back. "But it's the reason the liberal press is going to splash all over social media. In truth, we're trying to beat the Chinese to controlling the Nicaraguan Canal."

That piqued Daniel's interest because Cris's encampment was in the direct path of the canal that would connect the Caribbean Sea to the Pacific Ocean. It was common knowledge that with the increased size of modern ships, the Panama Canal was too narrow for their passage. Then there was the fact that the country of Panama was not on the best of terms with the United States of America since the U.S.A. gave them back control of the aging monstrosity.

"What happened to the Chinese billionaire who was funding the construction?" The last Daniel had heard, much of the pre-work had already been completed, and the next phase was to begin almost immediately.

"I doubt you follow international finance as closely as Katlin, but in the past two years the Chinese economy has tanked, so those billions have shrunk considerably." The corners of his mouth twitched up. "On the other hand, since the election the U.S. economy has taken bold steps forward. Our current politicians are more than willing to help Nicaragua connect the Atlantic and Pacific oceans, especially if we can have some control over who goes through that man-made channel."

Now it all started to make sense. When Cris had returned from earning a master's degree in oceanography in the United States, he had been very vocal about the Chinese plan. A price had been put on his head, so he'd gone into hiding in the mountains along with hundreds of other highly educated men who disagreed with the current government's policies. To protect themselves, and everyone else in hiding, Cris had learned military skills. That was one of the reasons Daniel was so readily accepted into the group. They could tell he was intelligent and offered the others training in survival skills. Cris was an avid reader and had immersed himself in books about military tactics. The man was a natural leader. In the four years Daniel had known him, Cris had practically transformed from a student activist to a calculating military tactician.

Tom threw back the last of the scotch. "I'm exhausted, and I know you must be too." He stood and set the empty glass on the coffee table. "I'd like you to spend the night here rather than over at the hotel. I have several more things I need to go over with you in the morning, but I need to catch a few hours of shut-eye first."

"I'd planned to sleep in my room upstairs." Daniel made

the last-minute decision. As drunk as everyone had been when he'd left, they'd all be sleeping in well past noon. Besides, when he told them the good news, they wouldn't give a shit where he'd been. He'd be a fucking hero.

As he trudged up his side of the double grand staircase, the fact that the last time he'd been there, Nita had been plastered to his side, hit him. They had talked almost all night before deciding they needed to get at least a power nap before she flew out in the morning. As he walked down the long hallway, he passed the room she had claimed as her own when joining the Ladies of Black Swan. He wondered if it still smelled like her? Had she been there recently? He resisted the urge to open the door to see if any remnant of her lingered.

Forcing himself to step beyond her door, and the next two along the hall, he finally reached his suite at the very end. Opening the double doors, he stepped into masculine luxury. The sensation of being home washed through him, chasing away the darkness from living in the shadow world. This was real. Life back in the guerrilla camp was who and what he pretended to be in order to get the job done. Here was the real Daniel Callahan's life.

His suite stretched the entire length of the house, more than twice the size of the others that lined the hallway. It was basically two rooms divided by a huge master bathroom that boasted a Jacuzzi tub big enough for company as well as a glassed-in shower with eight separate heads. The Jack and Jill style offered a second sink and toilet to be closed off from the bathing portion yet open to the living room side.

Daniel walked into the bedroom side and onto the large balcony. The quarter moon in a cloudless night made the curve of beach sparkle like amethyst crystals. He inhaled the clean ocean air and relaxed. Watching the sunrise over the

Caribbean Sea from his bed was one of his favorite things. He promised himself he'd sit out there staring at the turquoise water while sipping his morning coffee. He truly missed this life.

Wanting just a little more scotch before he crawled into bed, he went to the other half of the suite that faced the jungle. It also had a balcony that Daniel found he rarely used. Living day to day in the dense, humid vegetation took away the beauty of the wildlife and the uniqueness of a Central American jungle. After splashing two fingers of scotch into a glass, he stretched out in the comfortable seating area with his feet kicked up on the coffee table. Picking up the remote, he flipped through a hundred channels before settling in to watch an American football game on the man-sized flat screen TV.

Half an hour later, he turned off the game and headed straight for a hot shower.

Naked, he slid between the soft sheets and settled into the comfortable bed. It was lavish compared to the tent he lived in at the camp. Not for the first time, Daniel wondered what the hell he was doing with his life. He and the man at the other end of the hall owned the successful resort five hundred yards down the beach. He could live in the penthouse; sleep in comfort every night; have gourmet meals catered to his room; and his choice of clean, beautiful women that rotated with the tourist buses every week.

Yet, he would get up tomorrow morning, have breakfast with his uncle, confirm his new orders, and hike back the five miles to where he'd left the dirt bike. He'd straddle the ancient machine that shook his balls numb and take the well-worn path back to the hidden Nicaraguan camp where showering was an extravagance few ever decided to partake in, and food was often scarce. His army cot and sleeping bag were so far removed from the thousand-count sheets he slept on in Costa Rica there was absolutely no comparison.

At thirty-eight years old, Daniel was getting too old for this shit.

If Cris participated in the coup, Daniel might finally be able to leave Nicaragua...for good.

He would never take another deep undercover assignment again.

He couldn't.

CHAPTER 3

"GOOD MORNING, LADIES," GENERAL LYON, THE DIRECTOR of USSOCOM greeted the Ladies of Black Swan via video conference call. "The timetable for the Nicaraguan coup has been moved up. Before it begins, I have a mission for you."

In Lady Harrier mode, Nita glanced around the makeshift conference table at her teammates, then up at the large screen. She and her team, all active duty military from different services, ultimately reported to the Army general in charge of US Special Operations Command, even though they had been assigned to the Department of Homeland Security, Section 7 upon graduating from the Joint All-Female Special Operations School. It was nice not being under the thumb of Jack Ashworth for this mission. The DHS director of operations had an unhealthy fascination with their team leader which could be construed as sexual harassment. Nita was just glad to be under a military command once again.

Nita had enjoyed the past month, living on a remote military base in Honduras training both men and women, all Nicaraguan rebels. She was the backup physician for the clinic, but much preferred the hands-on action of teaching hand-to-hand combat, weaponry, and field first-aid.

That time had ended, apparently.

"Lady Harrier, are you familiar with level eight clean room procedures?" The general's question threw her for a moment.

"Yes, sir." Nita wondered where their assignment was sending them. All of her teammates looked at her with questions in their eyes.

"Excellent." The general leaned forward, and his desk chair squealed. "I don't need to tell any of you this information is top-secret. Four months ago, Ebola hit a small village in northeastern Nicaragua hard and fast. It nearly wiped out the entire population in days. Lady Harrier, are you familiar with the Reston strain of Ebola?"

"Yes, sir." She cocked her head. "But that's the only one of the five known Ebola viruses that doesn't spread to humans."

"Not anymore," he announced.

"Oh, fuck." The quiet words slipped out of Nita's mouth before she could rein them in.

"Educate us," the general ordered. "All I was told by the Centers for Disease Control was that if these live viruses get into the wrong hands they can wipe out an entire country in weeks, and there isn't fuck we can do about it. It's biological warfare at its finest, or worst, depending on your point of view."

Nita took a deep breath and gathered everything she remembered. "While I was in med school rotations, I was working in the lab when the monkeys in a Reston, Virginia lab started dying. We did some of the research ourselves at the United States Army Medical Research Institute of Infectious Diseases at Fort Dietrich in Maryland. It was concluded that the monkeys had both this unusual Ebola virus and hemorrhagic fever at the same time."

She shifted in the uncomfortable folding chair. "When other species of monkeys started to die—ones that were kept completely separate and had no direct contact with the infected monkeys—we figured out it was an airborne virus. But it didn't spread to humans."

General Lyon picked up his cup of coffee and sipped. "According to the CDC, humans can now be infected by the Reston Ebola virus. In conjunction with the World Health Organization, they have set up a lab inside the presidential residence in Nicaragua." He chuckled. "The president is so paranoid, he has his own hospital room and laboratory in the basement of his palatial estate. Everyone agreed it would be the most secure location in all of Nicaragua. They're about to be wrong."

The high, shrill squeal started as soon as General Lyon leaned back. Even Nita couldn't withhold the wince. "Ladies, I'm sending you in because several of the viral specialists are women. I think the five of you are the best choice to extract them to safety." He looked over his shoulder as though he was listening to someone out of range of the microphone.

Thirty seconds later, his attention returned to the screen. "We have a new development. Patching in CIA Deputy Director Thomas Gilpatrick."

Nita and her friends exchanged a glance. Katlin Callahan, their team leader, shrugged. Obviously, she didn't know what was going on even though Tom was her uncle.

"Splitting screen now, connecting in D.D. Gilpatrick." Lei Lu, the team's computer guru, clicked away on her keyboard.

"Ladies, nice to see you again. I wish it was under better circumstances." In private, all the women on the team called him Uncle Tom. They had been to his house for cookouts and seven course meals during their down time. He was like a favorite uncle to them all.

"Tom, what do you have for us?" The general's demand was cordial.

"A place to take the scientists." He grinned. "And a brand-new level ten clean room. I've also secured a transport mechanism that will assure no leakage."

"Thank Christ." General Lyon let out a long breath. "Now please tell me it's not going to be sent to the United States."

Tom's grin grew. "I think Costa Rica is far enough away, don't you?"

"Unc—" Katlin caught herself before she finished the word. "Deputy Director, sir, are we to take them to the Calla—"

"No, Lady Hawk. A modular clean room is under construction as we speak on the resort property down the beach from the site you're referring to." Tom spoke in code.

All the Ladies of Black Swan knew Tom along with Katlin's brother, Daniel, owned the resort. But no one knew how good General Lyon's intel was or whether he was aware of any of those connections.

"Sounds like a plan." The general signaled and someone handed him a piece of paper. As he signed it, he informed everyone on the call, "Ladies, I want you in there tomorrow night. Take the scientists to the resort in Barra del Colorado. I'm sure they'll be able to find rooms at the resort, don't you agree, Tom?"

Well, that confirmed General Lyons intelligence arm was superior to that at Section 7. Jack Ashworth hadn't known about the property Katlin and her family owned in Costa Rica.

The man with stars on his collar handed the sheet back to someone then leaned his forearms on the desk. "I'm dedicating a helicopter and crew to assist you in evacuating the scientists."

"Thank you, sir," Katlin quickly added. "It'll make our job a lot easier."

The corner of the general's mouth twitched. "Play nice, ladies. SOCOM, out."

Before anyone had time to question the general's last comment, Tom filled the screen. "In about six hours, I want you all to go to the clinic in your camp. Nita, there is a special package for you in the restocking delivery that should arrive shortly. During the original Reston outbreak, there were four workers who survived. The CDC has created what they hope will be a protective vaccine for this new strain of Ebola. I want you to inoculate each member of your team." One corner of his mouth kicked up. "Take the rest with you. I think you're going to need it."

"Will do, Uncle Tom." Nita nodded. She'd read his hidden message. "Does that mean they might need a booster shot once exposed?"

"It means you need to take the rest of it with you." Tom's answer was a non-answer.

"Will we see you in Costa Rica?" Katlin asked.

"Most likely." Tom nodded. "I'm just really hoping this coup isn't the cluster fuck I'm afraid it's going to be. We need to get all American assets out of that country before the shit hits the fan."

"What about Daniel?" Nita and Katlin asked at the same time.

Katlin gave her the briefest glance before returning her gaze to the screen.

"Daniel has a job to do, and he'll do it." Tom had morphed into one of the most powerful men in the CIA, leaving the jovial proxy uncle behind. He forced a smile.

"Just as I know you'll do yours. D.D. CIA out." The transmission ended.

"Play nice?" Nita raised one eyebrow as she looked at the perplexed faces of the other members of her team.

"Please, don't tell me they sent in Jonathan's team." Katlin referred to one of the all-male teams in Section 7 that despised the Ladies of Black Swan. She stood and stretched. "If it is, we'll deal."

Katlin's satellite phone rang. She took it out of her cargo pocket and checked the caller ID. "I think we should all hear this." She handed the phone to Lei Lu who connected it to her computer.

"This is Lady Hawk. Line is secure," Katlin announced when given the signal.

"Lady Hawk, this is operations. Meet the helicopter at 0230. Your team only. I repeat, your team only. Chopper is to be immediately hidden next to Black Swan jet."

"Operations, confirming. My entire team is required to be there?" Lady Hawk looked each woman in the eye before moving on to the next.

"Yes, ma'am. Those are your orders."

"Understood." She then added, "Who is my contact?"

There was a long pause while the only thing that could be heard was the clicking of keys. "Ma'am, I don't seem to have that information. Wait one." He returned to the line almost immediately. "I have no further information I can give you. Operations out."

"Well, that was abrupt," Tori noted and came to her feet.

"I call bullshit." Nita stood. "They just don't want us to know which assholes they sent us."

Lei Lu started gathering her computer equipment and handed Katlin back her sat phone. "I suggest we all go take a nap, because I'm quite sure we're going to be up most of the night."

"Good idea," Katlin agreed. "I need to tell air traffic control what's happening and make sure they clear the runway of all personnel after 0130."

"I think I'll take a few minutes of downtime and text Griffin." Grace had that goofy grin on her face, again.

Nita didn't understand how her friend could have committed herself to one man, and only one man. They weren't engaged or anything other than committed to a monogamous relationship.

Katlin, on the other hand, was engaged, so Nita understood monogamy in her case. She just hoped Alex Wolf understood what that meant. If he hurt her friend, Nita would have to permanently disable the man.

Nita glanced at her team leader's bare left hand. The very pretty diamond ring Alex had given her most likely was on the titanium necklace around Katlin's neck. They made an awesome couple. It was as though they had been together for years and years. They understood each other with a glance. They transformed each other from the hardass commanding officers into the most unique partnership Nita had ever seen. The give-and-take they demonstrated was intriguing. It was as though they enjoyed filling the other's needs. Strange. Nita had never seen a relationship like theirs up close and personal before. All she'd ever known was the give, give, give of her mother to her absent father.

But if Alex broke Katlin's heart, Nita wouldn't hesitate to cut off his balls.

Until then, they made a cute couple.

Nita preferred to play the field. She enjoyed men. Lots of them. Sometimes, two at a time. She grinned. Double the pleasure, double the fun.

As she walked back to her tent, she wondered why then had she turned down the two SEAL lieutenants at the cantina last weekend? They'd been fun. They all had the night off, the open-air bar was delightful, full-power alcohol rather than the watered down shit they served on the temporary base camp, had made for a perfect pickup place. Automatically, the officers congregated separately. During a uproarious game of Trivial Pursuit, she and her newfound frog friends had decimated the competition. But when they offered to continue their fun and games down by the ocean, images of Daniel stopped her from taking them up on their offer. She couldn't move past the way he'd leaned into her, capturing her mouth with his. Memories of the way the kiss started oh so gentle before they both lost control had kept her from a sexually gratifying night with two SEALs.

She hadn't wanted to be with any other man, even for the release and sexual gratification, since the night she and Daniel had done nothing more than talk. Well, there was that kiss.

Katlin's words tore her away from her sweet memories. "Nita, why don't you check and see what time the special shipment is to arrive at the clinic."

"I'm on it." Nita headed for the clinic.

All five Ladies of Black Swan stood on the tarmac at the hastily built airfield about a mile from the Honduran base camp. They were the only people around. Katlin had even sent away the guards who protected the team's sleek black jet hidden inside a new hangar a hundred feet away.

"According to the tracking code the ops center gave us, they're getting close and coming in fast." Too fast for a helicopter. Nita looked up at her team leader. "I distinctly remember you asking for a chopper. Is there any chance they're sending us an Osprey?" She handed Katlin the tablet.

"That has to be a fixed wing. It's traveling too fast to be a helicopter," Tori noted from Katlin's other side.

"Tracking codes confirmed." Lei Lu turned her computer around so the others could see.

Katlin shrugged. "I'm sure they're sending us what they think we need."

"We should be hearing it by now." Nita wasn't telling the others anything they didn't already know.

"I'm surprised we haven't heard—" Before Grace could finish her sentence, all five com units crackled.

"Black Swan team one, this is Black Swan team two on approach." The feminine voice wasn't what caused the shock on her teammates' faces.

What the fuck?

Katlin, now in Lady Hawk persona, was the first to reply, "Black Swan team two, this is Black Swan team one. How far out are you? Over."

All five women looked from the tablet into the starry night sky. They saw nothing. They heard nothing but the normal jungle sounds of the night.

"Black Swan team one, light up the LZ. We're coming in hot and dark." Lack of running lights was probably the reason they hadn't seen the plane.

Lady Eagle jumped in. "Black Swan team two, are you being pursued? Can you identify?"

"Black Swan team one, this is a practice exercise for what we might encounter during the next mission."

"Understood, Black Swan team two." Lady Hawk asked, "ETA?"

"Black Swan team one, ETA is ninety seconds. We are at sixteen thousand feet and descending fast."

Lady Hawk touched the screen, and lights instantly lined the runway. "They have to be flying a fixed wing. We'd hear them if it were a helicopter." She stared down at the tablet in her hand. "Lei Lu, we might need to recalibrate this—"

A loud hum filled the air cutting off her words.

All five women looked up as they felt the distinct downdraft of a descending helicopter.

The light whir of rotating blades replaced the familiar *whump*, *whump*, *whump* as the wheels of a huge black helicopter touched down.

They had never seen it coming.

"Holy fuck." Lady Falcon's voice was only audible through Nita's earbud.

The machine in front of them was the size of a Sikorsky Black Hawk, but much quieter than the stealth helicopter, and breathtaking. The flat black exterior seemed to accent the angular lines. Aerodynamically, the chopper would cut through the air rather than pushing it aside like an airplane. As the nearly silent engines shut down, the two blades, one stacked on top of the other, stopped almost immediately rather than glide slower with each rotation.

"Well, that's new." Nita said what everyone was thinking. She turned to Lady Hawk. "Do you think they'll let me fly it?"

"Right after me." Her team leader watched the pilot's door with her hands on her hips.

The side door slid open soundlessly and three people jumped out, completely clad head to toe in black. Only the Ladies of Black Swan wore completely black flight suits.

The pilot and copilot emerged from the front doors,

dressed the same as the others. As they stood nearly blending in with the helicopter, it became obvious they were women.

They looked fucking formidable. A chill went through Nita. For the first time she realized how she and her teammates must look as they descend the steps of their jet. A pang of resentment flowed through her. Goddamn it, she and her team were the Ladies of Black Swan, not these imposters.

The new arrivals all looked toward the woman who had crawled out of the pilot seat. If Nita hadn't been looking right at her, she would've missed the slight nod. The one who seemed to be in charge lifted the flight helmet off her head and tucked it under her left arm. She smiled and walked toward Nita and her team.

All five had their hair pulled back into a bun at the base of their skull, military regulation style. They all wore nervous smiles.

Her team leader stepped forward, hand extended. "Lieutenant Commander Katlin Callahan, code name Lady Hawk."

The dark-haired woman seemingly in charge thrust her hand forward. "I'm Kayla Scarlatto, team leader. You're real." She laughed lightly. "What I mean is…" She seemed to search for the right words. "All during our training, we heard rumors about the Ladies of Black Swan, but no one thought you were real…well, until we were assigned this mission and designated Black Swan team two."

"Yeah, we're fucking real." Nita looked past the new arrivals at the amazing helicopter. "Who do I have to blow so I can fly that black baby?"

"Exchanging sex for favors is highly discouraged, Lieutenant Banks." General Lyon's voice came through her comm unit very clearly.

Oh, shit. Nita closed her eyes. She'd forgotten they were

still live with the ops center. She chastised herself for speaking without thinking, once again. She had an extremely bad habit of saying exactly what was on her mind, completely unfiltered. She needed to work on that. And her swearing. Someday.

"Sir, I didn't mean it literally. It's just a phrase." She tried to recoup some sense of dignity. "I would never—"

"Lady Harrier," the general interrupted. "I know you wouldn't. You wouldn't work for me if you did. Moving on, Ladies of Black Swan, all of you, Lady Hawk is mission commander. Get that helicopter inside and those hangar doors closed. Reset the guards around the runway, then I want you ladies to get some sleep. We'll videoconference in the morning."

"Yes, sir," ten female voices answered.

CHAPTER 4

DANIEL SAT IN THE BACKSEAT OF A 1960s DODGE. BY American standards the car would be an antique, but in Nicaragua, it was transportation. With the tip of the barrel sticking out the side window, he rested his hand at the ready on a brand-new M4 rifle. It had the sweetest scope Daniel had ever used, offering both night vision and infrared with the click of a switch.

Deliveries had rolled through camp for days making Cris giddy with his newfound power and money. He had become the hero of the upcoming coup, and Daniel had become indispensable.

Although he had held a high rank within the group from the day he walked into camp and decimated Cris's personal guards, Daniel was surprised that he'd been kept in the dark about the details of exactly how the military was going to take over the Nicaraguan government. But as a good soldier, he did what he was ordered to do.

That night, he was to accompany Cris, Emilio Bautista, and Hugo Vargas into Managua, the largest city in the country. The nation's capital held just over a million people.

Like most modern cities, it ran the gambit from expensive international hotels with hundreds of rooms and five-star cuisine, to room rentals for a few dollars a day. Foreigners enjoyed a few high-end, all-inclusive resorts next to the smaller of Nicaragua's two main lakes, Lago Xolotlan.

Daniel didn't think he'd be enjoying any of those comforts that night. Riding through the nearly empty streets at two thirty in the morning, he figured they were on a reconnaissance run. Maybe that meant the coup would take place soon. He should report the information to the operations center in Langley. This might be the perfect opportunity to use the new satellite phone Uncle Tom had hidden in one of the most recent shipments. It was a heavy sucker which probably reached some new satellite array and kept all the information even more secret.

He was surprised when Emilio pulled over to the curb and parked two blocks from the presidential residence. They sat in silence while Cris checked his phone several times before he said, "Roll the windows up, but leave them cracked one inch." He smiled. "The United States government seems to be missing more than guns and grenades lately." His laugh was loud and boisterous as he slapped Daniel on the shoulder. "I'm so glad you're on our side."

Keeping with his cover, Daniel replied, "It pays to have low friends in high places. I'm just glad my contact wanted to dump all those weapons fast and dirty." While he had Cris talking to him, Daniel decided to take a chance and ask, "So what's all this for? Are we here to watch a bombing?"

"Oh, Daniel, my friend, you think too small." He pulled a metal briefcase into his lap and entered the combination. He lifted the lid and revealed a sophisticated computer. "See these little red dots? They are military blockades. The city is virtually surrounded. No one gets in. No one gets out."

Holy fuck. It's happening. Right now. Daniel wished he had a way to contact someone back at the CIA, but sitting in a car next to Cristobal, there was no way in hell he could whip out his phone and call or text. He'd have to wait.

Cris pulled the top down slightly, covering his hands as he typed. When the computer pinged, the anticipation in the leader's face stirred with excitement.

"And so it begins." Cris reached into the large duffel bag at his feet and pulled out heavy duty sound suppressors like the kind used on a shooting range. He passed them out to every man in the car. Reaching back in the bag, he pulled out small boxes. "Take one."

Daniel lifted the surprisingly heavy box from Cris's hand and carefully tipped open the lid to find a small communication system including an earbud and wire microphone. In the covert world, there was high tech, leading edge, then there was bleeding edge. These small devices were definitely the latter. When he reached in to pull it out, Cris put a hand on his arm.

"Not yet." All eyes were riveted on their leader. "Keep them safe in these boxes until I tell you."

The computer dinged several times. As Cris read each message, his smile grew broader. "General Cortez's men have just secured the airport," he announced with glee. "The railways and television station are now under our control."

Daniel didn't miss the inclusive word *our*. Obviously, their leader had become part of the inner circle for the coup. That meant he'd done his job well.

Three rapid dings preceded their next instructions. "Get those sound suppressors on now." Cris began counting down from thirty.

Daniel set the heavy box containing the comm unit on his crotch. He wasn't sure what was about to happen, but hopefully the metal would protect his junk as well as the sensitive equipment inside.

He scanned the sky out the side window and listened for approaching jets. He heard nothing but the occasional car and the constant white noise caused by everything from buzzing overhead streetlights to air-conditioning units in the apartments above the shops…city sounds quieted only by the late hour.

Daniel's stomach muscles tightened with every decreasing number.

"Three…two…one."

Nothing.

Nothing happened. Daniel's brain automatically started counting. *T minus one…*

Only empty night sky filled his vision.

T minus two…T minus—

He never made it to three.

He'd been expecting the whistle of a large bomb descending to earth faster than the speed of sound, the shake of its impact followed by the concussion of the explosion. He was prepared for that after being in several war zones.

He wasn't ready for the midair, small burst of blinding light that seemed to generate from a hundred feet above the presidential residence. It looked as though a helicopter had been shot down by a rocket propelled grenade, but he'd heard no familiar *whump, whump* of rotor blades, and he'd been listening hard.

The explosion wasn't anywhere near as big as he'd expected, but the impact pushed down on his whole body, even through the old car which probably had twice as much steel as last year's model. It was as though a giant hand pressed his head into his shoulders and his ass into the seat cushions, compressing the air within his body, rather than throwing him back away from the epicenter.

Daniel looked down at his kinetic watch to note the exact moment of impact. The time was 4:49 a.m.

As soon as the blast wave passed, he forced air into his lungs. Needing the brain power, he hyperoxygenated by taking fast deep breaths.

He scanned the sky for falling debris and a fireball as he sent up a quick prayer for the souls lost aboard the helicopter which had to have been hit by an RPG. Staring at the general area of the first explosion, he waited for the gas tanks to detonate.

Nothing.

There was absolutely nothing in the sky.

Daniel took in his surroundings, shocked at how quiet the world seemed. He wondered if the impact had damaged his hearing so he removed the sound suppressors.

No. He wasn't wrong. There was no sound whatsoever.

The opening of the metal briefcase seemed deafening, and Cris's typing was as loud as a snare drum next to his ear.

Not a glimmer could be seen outside the car. The only light came from the screen in his leader's lap. Daniel stared overhead and suddenly the night sky seemed filled with stars. He remembered lying on his back in the boat on Smith Mountain Lake while night fishing with Gramps and attempting to count all the stars. He couldn't remember the last time he'd been to the family home on the Virginia lake. He wondered if Katlin had been there recently or, if like him, she'd been too busy to bother with a vacation.

Staring out the window in a car filled shoulder-to-shoulder with men and the smell of adrenalin mixed with stale cigarettes, Daniel promised himself if he ever got out of this alive, he'd take everyone he loved to the lake for some well-deserved R and R...and fun.

"Sound suppressors off." Cris's order brought him back to the present. "Comm units in your ears."

"Where are we headed?" Daniel pulled out his gun.

"My new office." Cris chuckled. "Third floor of the building next to the presidential residence." He looked over his shoulder at Daniel who was in charge of his personal protection crew. "Clear the building. Make sure there is no one inside."

Daniel nodded. He could do that. No problem. The building had been dark the entire time they'd sat waiting.

"Let's go," Cris commanded.

"Yes, sir," three male voices chorused as each readied his weapon, opened the door, and stepped out into pure darkness. In night camouflage, matte helmets, and shades of black face paint, the men disappeared as though absorbed in a pool of midnight paint.

Thank God for night vision goggles. Daniel took lead. With bent knees, M4 tucked into his shoulder, he crept through the darkest part of the night to the side door of the building. Without the electronic locks, it easily opened. He signaled the men to split up and start with the lowest floor clearing room by room while he and Cris headed up the stairs.

The guerilla group leader seemed to know exactly where he was going. He turned left after entering the floor and walked straight to the large double doors at the end of the hall. Looking at the key card pad, Cris laughed, and pushed the door open. Making himself at home behind the enormous Brazilian mahogany desk, he opened the briefcase once again and began to type.

Daniel checked every room connected to the large office,

and carefully peered through the drawn blinds. Even the birds in the trees were sleeping. Nicaragua would wake up in a few hours to a whole new government, one more friendly to the United States.

"I'm going to clear the rest of this floor," Daniel announced.

Cris's grunt was his only acknowledgement.

As he started down the long, wide hall, he opened every door, ready to shoot. Finally, his men verified they hadn't found anyone. The building was empty, as expected.

A vibration on Daniel's thigh reminded him about the CIA cell phone.

He slid into the next room, assuring it was empty before he flipped the phone open to read the text.

Help evacuate Americans on sublevel two of the Presidential Residence.

A schematic popped up showing a tunnel on sub level one connecting the two buildings so he wouldn't have to go outside and chance being caught by the men handling the removal of the president.

Several dots moved around on the screen, but Daniel didn't know if those were good guys or bad guys. He'd just stay away from all of them. "Men," he instructed through his comm unit, "protect Cris at all costs. I'm going to check out some suspicious activity outside. Stay away from all the windows so you don't guide the tangoes straight to Cris."

"Roger that," the three others replied.

He quietly slipped through the halls and tunnel to the building next door and down to sublevel two. As soon as he opened the door, the smell of hospital overwhelmed him. The walls and floors gleamed with cleanliness. The scent of chlorine bleach assaulted his nose.

The device in his hand showed five people in a room a

hundred feet ahead on the left. He flipped his NVGs to infrared mode and confirmed no other heat signatures in the area.

Without electricity, the palm scanner next to the door to the dark room wasn't going to stop anyone. Daniel confidently yanked on the door.

It didn't budge. Maybe there was a manual release somewhere. He flipped up his NVGs and clicked on his flashlight. Blinding light flooded the hall. Scanning for a mechanical override, his gaze stopped at the big red words. Containment Area. Quarantine. Bio Hazard.

Oh fuck!

Above the door, in even bigger red letters, was a sign declaring Clean Room.

Glancing back at the special phone, he saw that four of the people had grouped together at the back of the room and one was at the window to his right.

Jerking his light to the glass, all he saw at first glance was a white space suit and glare off the curved face shield. Moving closer, he looked into the face of an angel.

His angel. The cherubic round face with hazel eyes he'd seen in his dreams. The soft full lips he'd kissed, just once, but had fantasized wrapped around his stiff, pulsing cock as she sucked hard. The face he'd seen with his eyes closed as he jerked off just last night.

The woman he could never have, stared daggers back at him.

He saw his reflection in the glass and even he didn't recognize himself with the grease paint in full black ops gear.

Nita Banks never blinked as she raised her hand and pointed a gun at his chest.

CHAPTER 5

WELL FUCK! THAT'S ALL WE NEED.

Lady Harrier stared at the man dressed for black ops and wondered what the hell he wanted with the scientists. His uniform was a far cry from the jungle cammies worn by the presidential guards who made regular passes every twelve minutes. She'd entered the clean room between rounds and had planned to extricate everyone the same way.

She'd wondered if her team had turned the lights out, although it hadn't been part of the plan. Maybe the coup had started. If so, they really needed to get the hell out of there. They were at ground zero for bad shit to happen.

And to complicate things even further, her comm unit connecting her with both Black Swan teams had decided to die, and her cell phone didn't work in the basement. Trained to operate independently, she wasn't worried. She could complete her mission. Matter of fact, the power outage could make her job even easier.

Then this Rambo-wannabe showed up.

She'd left the researchers with her heavy-duty flashlight to finish packing the crates and watched the intruder from the back of the lab. When he'd tried to break in, she decided to put a stop to his exploration, and possibly him.

The bright light shining in her face all but blinded her. She pulled her gun and was going to shoot him because she didn't have time for his shit. They were on the clock and that fucking cool helicopter Black Swan team two flew was due back in twenty-seven minutes for first extraction attempt.

Stepping out of the glaring light, she watched his bright blue eyes widen when he saw the gun. She knew those beautiful eyes. A wide sapphire blue ring surrounded a crystalline blue, the color of the Caribbean Sea at thirty-five feet underwater. A third ring of silver next to the pupil amplified their intensity. Her team leader had those eyes.

So did her brother, Daniel.

Nita had stared into them with lust and unguarded desire on more than one occasion. The last time she'd seen them, Daniel had kissed her with so much passion, she'd wanted to throw him on the ground and see just where the ride would take them both. But the kiss had been far too short for that conclusion. She was headed back to the U.S.A.—with her team which included his sister—so their hidden kiss was brief, but filled with promise.

Their gazes met and a slash of white teeth gleamed amidst the night camouflage face paint. *Nita, let me in,* he mouthed.

Excitement and relief warred within her. Daniel was there.

She waved him over to the door. He had to suit up, for his safety. Half way to the non-functioning wind curtain, she veered off to grab her bag and the vials sent by Uncle Tom. She internally chuckled. Her surrogate uncle was Daniel's *real* uncle. But she had no familial feelings for the man who'd spent an entire night sharing views on every subject imaginable, getting to know her, the real Nita Banks. She had plenty of other emotions when it came to the hard-bodied CIA agent.

She shook her head as though that would wipe away any memories about the way his arms felt around her, his deep voice in her ear as he told her to sleep well while hugging her goodnight.

Focus, she chastised herself, *you have a mission to complete.*

She stripped out of the suit in the vestibule and stepped through the first area to unlock the door. When he stepped in, the smell of man and Daniel's unique scent filled the small area.

She wanted to throw her arms around him, but instead said, "You need to suit up. The CDC intern dropped a tray of live Ebola viruses when the lights went out. This strain is an airborne contagion."

"Oh, fuck." He headed for the dressing area.

"Wait." Nita pulled out a syringe and the bottle of what everyone hoped was a preventative. While filling the vial, she ordered, "Drop your pants."

The corners of his mouth twitched as he unbuckled his cargos. She could only imagine his thoughts, but was glad he didn't say anything.

"This goes into your butt cheek right near your hip so I don't need to see your dick." Although, maybe someday she'd like to see it…touch it…lick it…suck it.

"You keep looking at me like that, and I'll drop these pants right now and show you exactly what I can do with my dick."

She glanced at his crotch and sure enough, he was hard. It was probably just a combat boner. Men got them all the time when adrenalin rushed through their veins. She'd seen it many times while in theater, especially just as they headed into a stressful mission.

She shrugged. In her clinical voice, she claimed, "I have no idea what you're talking about, but as a doctor, I've seen lots of dicks before. Yours isn't anything special." She lied. He had a very impressive package if the bulge in his boxers was any indication.

She tore open an alcohol wipe and swabbed the area before trying to pull together some fat so the injection didn't hurt as much, but the man was fit. He didn't have an inch of fat on him. Just a nice tight ass. She tried to find a little more so this time she grabbed a handful creating a mound.

"A little pinch, then it'll feel warm for a minute." At least that's how hers had felt.

He didn't even flinch when she injected the needle and plunged the lifesaving liquid into his butt. A tiny drop of blood surfaced when she was finished, so she used the alcohol swab to remove it.

He pressed around the injection site. "That made a lump."

She swatted his hand away and kneaded the area hoping it would dissipate faster than hers had. "Rubbing might help."

He grabbed her wrist and lifted her hand away. His eyes closed and dragged in a deep breath. When they opened, powerful blue eyes, filled with controlled lust, stared back at her. "I'd much rather you rub something else, but this is not the place and most certainly, not the right time." He pried open her fisted fingers and placed a kiss on her opened palm. "But I promise you, Nita Banks, I'll let you touch and rub any part of my body when this fiasco is over." His grin was devilish. "As long as you let me return the favor."

She couldn't breathe. Tingles raced from her hand to her lungs and completely shut them down. Lack of oxygen. That's why her brain wasn't functioning correctly. Or was it the man who still gently held her hand in his much larger one?

Where the hell were all her snappy replies? She could always put a man in his place. But there was only one place she wanted this man. In her bed. Then she'd get tired of him like all the rest, and kick him to the curb.

"What makes you think I'd let you touch me?" She was already getting wet and aching between her legs at the thought of Daniel circling then rubbing her clit. She needed to shut this flirtation down right now, so she stepped away from him and discarded the needle. "Ew. That's a little incestuous. I thought you considered all of Katlin's friends as quasi-sisters."

He spun her around and pressed her body into his, jerking his hips into her lower belly. She couldn't miss the extraordinary erection. "There's no fucking way I think of you as a sister."

He crashed his mouth on hers.

The second his warm lips touched hers, her mind melted, completely forgetting they were in the midst of an op. He slanted his head and opened his mouth just as she opened hers, giving him access, taking the kiss deeper.

"Dr. Hall, we're pa— Oh, excuse me." The young voice was like dumping cold water on them.

Nita took a huge step away from Daniel and looked toward the lab entrance. What the fuck was she thinking, bantering with Daniel while the scientists were feverishly packing, scared out of their minds that they'd be captured and tortured? She'd spent valuable time reassuring them that she, a female, was going to get them to safety.

She stared at the woman. "You're ready to go?"

"Yes." The pretty young blonde in the third year of her

doctorate program couldn't take her eyes off Daniel. "Is he here to get us out?"

"Yes, ma'am," Daniel interjected before Nita could say no.

She glanced over her shoulder at him. Why the hell did she think he was there? Just to kiss her stupid? "You are?"

He nodded. "I was sent to this location to help evacuate American citizens." He opened what looked like an older flip phone and showed her the 3-D schematic with six red dots, three together in one place and three more at the back of the adjoining room.

"Does it show you where the rest of the Ladies of Black Swan are?" Nita stared at the device but only saw only the six of them.

"No. Somehow only you were tagged," he noted.

"Yeah. I tagged each of the researchers as soon as I got here so we could track them if we got separated." She wouldn't mention that she had an implanted tracker, just in case Daniel didn't know.

"What was your extraction plan?" he asked.

Irritated because he seemed to want to take over, she explained, "Our plan *is* to head out the door at the end of this hall. A tunnel one level up goes north. We escape through the adjoining building."

"Then what?"

"Follow me," she ordered. He didn't need to know all their plans. "You can help us carry the containers." She didn't bother re-suiting, but walked into the clean room. It was no longer germ free by then anyway. Without the backpressure ventilation system, the live viruses dropped by the intern were already seeping into the surrounding air, possibly traveling through the ventilation system, infecting everyone in the building. At least all the researchers, and Daniel, were protected...supposedly. She hoped the CDC back in Atlanta was right.

"Go ahead and get out of those suits." In full Lady Harrier mode, she ordered the scientists around like recruits. They immediately obeyed and shucked out of the self-contained hazard suits. "Let's go."

Each grabbing a milk crate-sized container and pulling the strap over their head, she led the way, weapon to her shoulder, scope on infrared.

"I've got your six." Daniel grabbed the last two containers allowing two of the researchers to walk unencumbered. A pang of jealousy shot through her when the young intern blushed as he took the strap from her hand.

The man oozed testosterone. But she knew exactly what the student felt.

They had just reached Sublevel 1 when they heard boots on the stairs, descending fast.

"Hurry," Daniel ordered in a low voice. "Get them into the tunnel. I'll take care of those guys."

Thankful he was there, Lady Harrier darted through the door into the pitch-black hall. As soon as the door shut, she instructed the nervous scientists, "Hang onto the waistband of the person in front of you. We're going to move fast."

Thank God for the night vision mode on her riflescope, but it was a straight shot to the next building.

Muffled gunshots echoed down the long hall as she trotted the hundred yards. "Everyone keeping up?"

"We're all here," the male researcher replied. "But the soldier..."

"Don't worry about him. He'll catch up." She didn't dare think about Daniel getting shot. She had to concentrate on getting these three women and one man to safety.

At the door on the far side, she halted. "Stay quiet while I check to see if the way is clear." With her hand on the knob, the door at the other end flew open.

Lady Harrier shoved the civilians behind her and took aim down the long hall.

"Nita, wait." Daniel's voice echoed as his running steps tapped on the concrete floor. "Don't open that door."

Relieved it was him, she remained in a shooting position, rifle aimed at the far door in case he was followed.

He wasn't even breathing hard when he reached her. "I have men in this building. Let me go in and be sure it's clear." He screwed in an earpiece then boldly opened the door.

In Spanish, he quickly ordered, "Lieutenant Callahan here, report in." Pause. "Stay on protection for Cris. I'm on Sublevel 1 and headed back outside to assist General Cortez's men. Stay away from the windows. Watch the hallways." Pause. "Roger that. Callahan out."

He stared at Nita. "Let's go."

With a nod to her, they sprinted the length of the hallway to the outside door. After checking to be sure no one was around, she led them through and into deep shadows. She sucked in a breath of fresh air as she took stock of her charges. The heavyweight man was winded, as were two of the women. The intern was obviously in much better shape. The way she smiled up at Daniel expectantly, as though for direction, infuriated Nita.

She was in charge. This was her mission. He'd appeared out of nowhere and seemed to take over. They were willing to follow him just because he had a penis. Well, that didn't work in the world of Black Swans. Everyone seemed to forget that, with a vagina, she could get all the penises she wanted! At that moment, she wanted to get rid of Daniel Callahan and his impressive package.

Without even a side-glance at the college student, he

strode to Nita's side while scanning the surrounding area. Tenderly, he tucked a stray curl behind her ear and traced her jaw with a finger. "Where to next, angel?"

Her mind was too overtaken with the sensations from his touch to even respond.

He bent to peer straight into her face. "You okay, Nita?"

She heard the true concern in his voice.

"Excuse me," the young intern interrupted. "I'm Chyna— that's with a *y*, not an *i*—and I just want to thank you for rescuing us." She threw her arms around Daniel's neck.

Immediately shattering her lust fog, Nita snapped, "Of course I'm okay." She turned away from the woman in Daniel's arms, and took her comm unit out then tapped it before placing it back in her ear. "Operations, this is Lady Harrier. Confirm connection."

Silence.

"What the fuck is wrong with this thing?" She took it out again and turned on her red light.

Daniel plucked it from her palm. "It's fried. The EMP took out everything electronic that wasn't hardened." Heat radiated from his body warming her entire side as he invaded her personal space. He'd obviously scraped off Chyna with a *y*.

Ignoring him, she slid out her phone, but couldn't even get it to power up. "Fuck!" she swore in a low tone.

Holding out his phone, he offered, "Mine works. I don't have USSOCOM's number, but if you need Katlin, press five."

"That'll do." She grabbed it and called her team leader.

"Great to hear from you, big bro, but I'm in the middle of a shit storm," Lady Hawk said hurriedly. "If you're in trouble, though, I'm here for you." Her tone had become apprehensive.

"It's Lady Harrier. Daniel lent me his phone," Nita explained.

"Thank Christ," her team leader said on a sigh. "That fucking EMP wiped out all our communications gear. Did it get your phone?"

"Yeah." She thought about the Black Swan team two helicopter that had dropped her off. "Is everyone safe?"

"Thank God the chopper was half way back to our base when the explosion happened. According to operations, you were at ground zero. It wiped out everything electrical within a two-mile radius, which included most of the city. Some electronics got slapped beyond that, but there's a lot of farmland once you get outside the city limits."

"Good to know." Nita needed to get moving before they were discovered. "Extraction point alpha in fifteen minutes?"

"Negative. We're in flight now. There's a park along the lakeshore. Can you be there in five?" Lady Hawk was already in flight. That was great news. Nita wasn't sure the scientists could make it the mile to the soccer stadium for extraction. She could see the park from where they stood.

"Roger that." Lady Harrier turned to Daniel only to realize that Chyna was wrapped around his free arm. "We're moving out. Now."

CHAPTER 6

WHAT THE HELL WAS UP WITH NITA? IF DANIEL DIDN'T KNOW better, he'd think she was jealous of the frightened young girl clamped to him. Being female, he would've thought Nita had more compassion. He'd been on more than one op where he'd rescued women and they were always frightened, on the verge of panic. He'd handle what's-her-name…Chastity…no, Chelsea…no, that wasn't it either. Aha, Chyna, with a y—like that fucking y was important at a time like this.

Nita walked back to the scientists huddled up against the building. "Can you see the lake at the bottom of the hill? That's where we're headed." She looked at Daniel. "I'll take point, and you bring up our six." To the anxious researchers she instructed, "We have to work our way through the park, but we'll use the trees as cover. I'll go first and Daniel will send you to me, one at a time. Understood?" She looked at each scientist for affirmation. "Line up."

They both tipped down their night vision goggles and searched the area. Over her shoulder she reminded them, "Do exactly as I do, one at a time, follow me."

She sprinted to the first large tree. At her signal, Daniel

sent the first researcher to her. As each was hidden, he'd send the next. When he stepped behind the last person, she took off for the next tree. They repeated this three times. After sending the second researcher, she signaled for him to hold. He followed the direction of her gaze, and froze.

Fuck. Ten fully armed members of the presidential guard were sweeping through the park as though looking for the tangoes responsible for capturing the president. Daniel looked at the innocent researchers and inwardly shuddered at the torture they would endure needlessly.

Nita had moved the first two researchers to the back of the large tree and had taken up a defensive position, gun pointed at the incoming troops. Fortunately, Daniel's two charges had no idea what was heading their way. In a low voice he ordered, "Move around to the back side and lay flat on the ground."

Chyna grabbed his gun arm. "But I'm supposed to run next," she said in a normal voice. He shoved her around the tree and pushed her head down as he tried to make his own body as small as possible, seconds before the first bullet nicked the tree, sending shards of bark in all directions.

Chyna squealed.

"Shut the fuck up," Daniel hissed through clenched teeth as he raised his rifle to his shoulder and took out two of the advancing men. From twenty feet away, he heard a burst of five bullets and watched three more men drop.

Damn, Nita can shoot.

Red tracers flew by on both sides of the tree as the park filled with the sound of a firefight. Fortunately, he and Nita had the high ground with more trees surrounding them.

Then everything went quiet.

Out of the corner of his eye, Daniel watched Nita pick up a pinecone and toss it down the hill behind a tree. Two men

popped out from behind a statue and ~
tree to fire into the lower are~
their bodies to Daniel. H~
the third.

What ~

B~

sp~
dow~

"~

"R~
man as C~

Nita w~
trees as muc~
sandy beach ~
researchers.

"Everyone d~
body as flat as you~
they'll be back with~
here."

Daniel heard whim~
researchers. Chyna was c~

Before either he or Nita~
older man in the group warne~
you get us all killed."

over the lake. He turned and was startled by the closeness of the helicopter. At least he thought it was a helicopter. The pointed nose and sharp angles looked like something out of a science fiction comic book rather than a U.S. military arsenal.

The whipping of the rotor wind around him was oddly comforting. It had always meant he was headed home after a mission. He sighed heavily as he looked back at the building where Cris and his guards were waiting. Disappointment fell over him like a pelting rain.

He wasn't going home.

But Nita and the scientists were.

As the side door slid open, he recognized the woman dressed head to toe in black, even though a helmet hid her long blond hair. He couldn't help but smile at his sister as he helped herd the scientists to the helicopter. When he lifted Chyna onto the deck of the chopper, he looked up into a copy of the same blue eyes he saw in the mirror every morning.

"Hey, sis. This is a new one for us." He could see the shock on her face before she broke into a broad smile. Jumping out of the helicopter, she threw her arms around him.

"Are you coming back to the compound with us?"

He hugged his sister. The yearning to go home intensified. He was so over this undercover shit. The next time he spoke to their Uncle Tom, he'd ask for an immediate transfer. Hell, he might just quit the CIA. He had so much more than just his future to think about now.

"Sorry, little one. I can't." But damn it, he wanted nothing more than to hop on that chopper with her and be drinking fine Scotch whiskey within hours, eating some of the most delicious food prepared by their cook, and to sleep in his big soft bed. But not tonight. "I'll try to sneak off and see you as soon as possible." That was as much a promise to himself as it was to her.

The dual blades on top of the helicopter started to increase speed.

"Sorry, big bro. Gotta go. Stay safe." She leaped into the futuristic-looking helicopter, then she turned to wave. Nita stepped up beside her and mouthed *thank you* while saying it in American Sign Language.

He placed his fingers on his pursed lips and flung them toward the helicopter as it lifted off, throwing a kiss. To which woman, he wasn't sure.

The helicopter shot almost straight up and quickly disappeared in the dark of the night as though it had never been there. Once he was sure they were safely gone, Daniel trotted back toward the office Cris had appropriated. He announced himself as he approached his men who still stood guard on either side of the door to their leader.

"Any problems?" Daniel asked.

"None. But we did hear shooting," Emilio noted.

"Yeah, we got the bastards." Daniel wasn't about to define which bastards he was referring to, but instead strode into the office where Cris sat behind the computer.

"We're leaving," the leader said a few minutes later as he unhooked a cable to the PC sitting on top of the desk. "The city is officially dead."

"What the fuck?" Daniel glanced up to find the guerrilla leader grinning proudly.

"What the EMP didn't take out, I just virtually destroyed. It will take years to rebuild this city." The two men stared at each other for a long moment before Cris explained. "We're building a whole new capitol at San Miguelito on Lago Cocibolca. General Cortez plans to wipe out Managua, literally scraping away everything from the former regime."

Daniel considered the small port on the largest lake in Nicaragua and couldn't help asking, "Why there? That's nothing but a tiny fishing port."

Cris clicked the locks on the metal briefcase. "In five years, it will be the halfway point of the Nicaraguan Canal linking the Atlantic and Pacific oceans. World-class hotels and high-end resorts will replace those fishing shacks. People from all over the world will get off cruise ships and spend their foreign dollars in the most modern city in Central America. Ships that are too big for the Panama Canal will easily fit through the canal that I am building. Commercial boats from every country around the world will pay us to travel the length of my canal."

Daniel didn't miss the word *my*. Cris had studied ocean engineering in the United States and possessed a master's degree in the field, but upon returning to Nicaragua, he had not been allowed to work on the fledgling idea of a transcontinental canal. The now previous president hadn't found a billionaire who was willing to part with enough of his money to buy off the rights to dig the canal across Nicaragua. By the looks of things, General Cortez didn't have that problem.

Cris picked up the briefcase and headed toward the door. "San Miguelito will be one of the richest fresh water ports in the world. Tourists will spend millions of dollars every day enjoying international cuisine, the finest hotels in the world, and our beautiful lake, all because of my canal."

At the double doors to the office he stopped and turned around to face Daniel. "Nicaragua will no longer be the Third World shit hole the U.S. president called it. We will be a powerful nation. There will be plenty of money for health care, education, and new roads." Cris smiled. "Did I tell you about my railroad we're building at the same time as the canal? We will control the fastest East-West commerce shipment in the world. And that magnificent fleet of warships the United States uses to threaten the world with will protect us."

He slapped his hand on Daniel's shoulder. "And you'll be there, right beside me, my friend. But now we need to return to camp while General Cortez deals with the fallout from his takeover. I feel like fucking every woman there." His grin fell. "Every woman except for my sister. She's yours."

Daniel thought about the bitch he'd used to get close to Cristobal Maximo four years ago. On the outside, she had been beautiful with dark golden eyes, long black hair, and large lips around perfect teeth. Too bad the woman was certifiably crazy. And paranoid. And a slut.

She'd been educated in the U.S.A. like her brother. But underneath that sorority polish was a scheming bitch who'd fuck any man to get her way. She soon discovered that Daniel was not the jealous type. They'd never been married although she'd tried twice to tie him to her forever. He knew better than to shackle himself to a deceitful, cunning woman who would kill him as quickly as she'd suck his cock. She needed to be the constant center of attention and always in control.

Daniel didn't play that way so they'd fought loud and often. But damn, the makeup sex was unbelievable. She'd always come back to him, apologizing for whatever she'd concocted in that insane brain of hers—because she was truly, fucking crazy. The shit she'd come up with was literally insane.

Thank Christ her brother knew just how deranged she was. Sometimes Daniel thought Cris "gave" her to him so someone else would have to put up with her shit and handle her mood swings. Daniel was never sure if she was on drugs, or should be. All he knew for sure was that she was dangerous so he'd kept his distance, most of the time. But like an addictive drug, when he was at his lowest, she'd show up and offer him relief. He'd take what she offered, hating himself afterward for it.

Tonight, with Nita on his mind and his emotions out of control for the doctor who haunted his dreams, there was no way he could bury himself inside any other woman, especially the crazy bitch. He wanted to take the Land Rover and point it toward Costa Rica. He was afraid if he did that tonight, he might never come back. And he had to come back.

Instead, Daniel got drunk with his men—the two dozen elite, highly trained, and most intelligent soldiers in the camp. Just before dawn, he'd crawled into bed, alone.

Daniel slept through much of the next day, exhausted from the night in Managua. Still feeling like shit, he briefly dragged himself out of bed, and managed to check on everything he was responsible for. Scarfing down some lunch, he watched the camp children play, bringing joy to his tortured soul for their now-brighter future. The guards on duty assured him Cris was safe and obviously contented by the number of women who'd been in his bed since their homecoming. Satisfied everything was as it should be, Daniel returned to bed.

By the second day, he was feeling human once again. He dropped by the barracks to roust the man who'd been on the mission with him. He wanted to do some reconnaissance back in Managua. "Rise and shine," he bellowed next to his bunks.

When Hugo Vargas rolled over, he looked terrible and smelled worse. "Sorry, lieutenant. There must have been something in that whisky last night."

"You hit the bottle again last night knowing you were on duty today?" Daniel was pissed that his man would shirk his duties in such a way.

"That wasn't last night, sir. It's been two days," the man next to him pointed out.

"Yeah, lieutenant, we've been throwing up for two days now," another soldier tried to explain.

Daniel looked at his watch. That date couldn't be right. He hadn't slept for an entire day and night. Somehow, he'd lost a whole twenty-four hours. Had that fucking bitch, Cris's sister, drugged him again? She'd done that to him once, and made him late for meeting Katlin at their compound in Costa Rica. He smiled deep inside as he remembered that visit. He'd never forget kissing Nita for the first time.

Just then one of the men shot out of the bed and dragged his weakened body to the bathroom. Sounds of dry heaves filled the long barracks.

"I'll send in the camp medic," he promised as he left to check on Cris.

On his way through the tents, Daniel saw the man who had been designated camp doc. Although he'd never finished more than two years of med school, he had mad skills at bullet removal and could stitch sutures like a plastic surgeon. Daniel could attest first hand to both abilities.

"Hey, doc, can you check on my men? They're puking their guts out." Daniel looked at the harried older man.

"Them and half the camp." The medic shook his head. "Seems we have the flu making its way through our little village. It's been hitting people harder than usual, though."

"Help us." Down the dirt street, a young teenager half-carried an older woman who looked to be her grandmother.

"The farmers around us are bringing their sick here to see me." He looked up at Daniel. "And there's not a fucking thing I can do for any of them. We just don't have the supplies." As though an idea dawned, he looked up at Daniel hopefully once again. "Do you think you can get medicine in here from your contacts? Maybe something for flu? I could really use gallons of rehydration fluids. And potassium. Their joints and muscles seem to ache, but that could be due to the high fever. Which reminds me, we're desperately low on aspirin to bring down the fevers. Do you think you can help?"

Daniel wasn't sure, but he'd run the request up the chain of command. "I'll see what I can do." He glanced around the area looking for the small familiar faces. "Where are all the children?"

"When people started getting sick, the teacher took them to the school." The doctor gave him a weak smile. "Thanks to you, they all got their flu shots this year. But we all know that's not a guarantee they won't get sick."

With a short nod, Daniel headed toward one of the few adobe buildings located on the outskirts of the camp. He was more than a little concerned, especially for the babies.

CHAPTER 7

Nita was more exhausted than she had been during Hell Week, the final test of their SEAL training, as she dragged her tired ass from the clean room located on the resort property next door to the Callahan compound in Costa Rica. Even though everything they needed had been delivered, the lab still had to be completely set up before they could release the live viruses into the new storage units. Complicating the process to the nth degree was the fact they had to do everything in self-contained clean suits. It was like walking around in a bulky space suit with a set of heavy scuba tanks strapped on.

Originally built to be a beachside grill that could withstand a category five hurricane, the large block building was certainly stout. It had its own water source and HVAC separate from the hotel. To ensure containment, a U.S. company specializing in mobile clean rooms had brought in their panelized system, totally encasing the interior and creating a leading edge facility.

Uncle Tom had insisted that every piece of equipment be hardened against another EMP, which included the air conditioning systems as well as backup generators for the backup generators. When the Ladies of Black Swan had arrived three days ago, the clean room itself had been completed, but the air systems were still under construction. Thank God somebody was smart enough to put several filters in place, as well as bacteria killing lights, within the ventilation. But all of that had taken time.

The scientists had just confirmed that Reston Ebola was an airborne virus and simple breathing could transmit the illness. It could penetrate through the mucus in the eyes and nose. This virus was one of the most dangerous on the planet.

Nita yearned for a solid six hours between soft sheets as she trudged over the well-worn path in fresh scrubs and a new pair of flip-flops. Her mind spun with too many possibilities to rest so she hung the right and walked along the sandy beach, allowing the lap of waves and warm sea breeze to calm her. Stretching out on one of the comfortable lounge chairs, she stared at the winking stars in the moonless sky.

She forced fresh salt air all the way to the bottom of her lungs to purify every corner of the recycled air she'd been breathing for days. As she had learned in yoga class, she let her muscles relax one-by-one. She never remembered reducing the tension in her calves.

The distant sound of a fussy baby brought Nita to her nightmare. Red glowed beneath the child's chocolate skin. *What the hell am I missing?* The panicked thought raced through her mind once again, just as it had so many times since her last year in med school. She had delivered this precious life into the world on OB/GYN rotation. The newborn's Apgar scores were ten-by-ten, excellent on anyone's scale. Less than twenty-four hours later, the child had been moved to the neonatal intensive care unit and the mother had disappeared.

The supervising NICU physician had assured Nita that they had run every test possible, but had yet to discover why the child ran such a high fever. Wanting nothing more than to pull the baby from the hard plastic encasement, Nita had satisfied her need by running a gloved hand down the small hot cheek. She had to be missing something. She'd retracted her hands back through the protected circles and grabbed the file at the end of the tiny bed. Accustomed to looking at lab results, she scanned the long list of numbers. Damnably, nothing had stood out.

Her gaze had swept the many machines connected to the small body clad only in a diaper. *What the fuck am I missing?*

The baby's cries had quieted as her legs and arms calmed as though she'd run out of energy. Nita had watched the elevated heart rate drop to one of sleep. The tiny chest had expanded and contracted several times. Satisfied the unnamed child would rest, she had gone on with her rounds.

Near the end of her shift, after delivering eight more babies, Nita had decided to drop into the NICU one last time before heading back to the barracks. The second she stepped in the door, her entire body had tensed.

The physician in charge of neonatology had stood over the opened incubator, tiny electrical probes in hand as a solid-tone alarm pierced the air. "Clear." The nurses surrounding the crib had all lifted their hands. A second later, the heart machine had blipped a normal cadence. "We've got her back." He'd scanned the machines before giving orders changing the medications.

Nita had walked over and stood on the other side of the clear plastic crib. A nurse had handed her a pair of gloves, and she'd deftly slid her fingers into the latex. "Have you figured out what's wrong with her?"

The Army colonel had glanced up from the chart to meet

her eyes. "Sometimes we never know, Lieutenant Banks. This one has me baffled. I wish the mother was here to give us more information." He flipped the hardcover over the chart and returned it to its position at the bottom of the bed. With only the tilt of his head, he'd asked her to join him. As the nurses encapsulated the baby once again, checking all the tubes and machines, the older doctor had led Nita to the far side of the room.

The muffled cries of a small baby had seemed so real as Nita's nightmare continued.

Quietly the senior officer had confessed, "I hate losing any patient, but I hate it even more when the mother just dumps the baby on us and disappears. I sent the MPs after her. The address she gave is an empty apartment. Her husband has been stationed at one of the forward operating bases in Iraq for nearly a year. We sent a message to him, but I doubt the child is his. Probably why she bolted."

Nita wasn't sure who she felt worse for, the baby struggling for life or the young enlisted man married to the cheating bitch who had abandoned her infant.

In the back of her mind, she'd known it had been days, but in the horrible dream it was only a second. She was back in the NICU.

The baby's condition had continued to decline. The colonel had sent her records off to several specialists in the neonatology field, and the hospital had conducted a dozen more tests, all to no avail. Her tiny heart had stopped multiple times, but they had been able to revive her.

She'd held the child next to her chest, rocking in the chair beside the incubator when tiny brown eyes opened and looked directly into hers. Nita had sworn she saw a smile. The baby had exhaled long and smooth as it closed its eyes and went limp in Nita's arms.

Dreading the next scene, Nita tried to force herself awake. The ending never changed.

She heard the colonel say, "Nita, I need your help."

No, that's not what the colonel had said. He had started barking orders for the crash cart.

"Nita, wake up, angel. I need your help." The senior military officer's voice didn't sound quite right, but the words weren't right either. He had never called her angel. That kind of familiarity was very much against regulations. The only person who called her angel was...

"Angel, I need you to wake up."

She forced her eyes open and stared into Daniel Callahan's bright blue eyes.

The baby from her dream whimpered. She certainly didn't want to go back there.

Taking a deep breath, she focused on the dark-tanned man leaning over her. "Daniel, what the hell you doing here?"

"I need your help." He thrust a baby into her arms. "Isabella is sick, and there's no more medicine in camp."

Heat poured off the child even through the light baby blanket as it shook its fists and kicked tiny legs. The stench of sour milk and diarrhea assaulted Nita's nasal passages. She wanted to drop the child and run as far and fast as she could.

She didn't do babies.

As she swung her legs over the side of the lounge, the child started to calm. Nita would just hand this baby back to Daniel and someone else could deal with it. His sister was inside and she'd always wanted a child but couldn't have one of her own. Perhaps Katlin could take care of it. Grace was really good with kids. The three of them could handle this infant. The child wasn't Nita's problem.

Standing toe-to-toe with Daniel, Nita couldn't help but look into the tiny face as it exhaled a long slow breath. The baby gazed at her with the same crystalline blue eyes as the man only inches away.

"You have to save my Bella." The plea in Daniel's voice shot straight to Nita's soul, and the wall she'd built around her heart shook with the force of an earthquake.

She was holding Daniel's baby.

A tempest of sensations screamed through her. The reality in her arms contradicted the heat in his kiss just days ago. Was he married? She glanced at the ring finger on his left hand and saw it empty, neither an untanned band nor indentation from a long-worn ring. But to have two children, he must be in some kind of committed relationship. She glanced between the two children looking for similarities. Could they have two different mothers? Nita couldn't tell if the same woman had given birth to both children. Perhaps Daniel was not the man she had thought he was. Was he just like her own father? Nothing more than a sperm donor.

Longing for the father she never had, forced childhood memories to surface. As soon as she'd been old enough to realize her biological father would never be her dad—could never truly be part of her life because he had the perfect family who lived in the next town over—Nita had vowed never to repeat her mother's mistakes. She would certainly not fall in love with a man whose heart, and time, belonged to another woman and his children he'd created with her. She carefully guarded her heart so no man would ever capture it. That's why she rarely spent more than one night with any man. The long-term emotional pain just wasn't worth the physical gratification.

Daniel Callahan wasn't worth another minute of her time. He'd gotten too close. After their all-night confessional, he knew her better than any man ever had. He knew her weaknesses. The kisses they had recently shared had seeped into the mortar of the wall she'd built around her heart and had started to dissolve the very foundation. She couldn't allow that.

Shoving the baby back into Daniel's arms, disgust at his lie of omission after all they'd shared for hours won over all the other emotions churning through her. How could he not tell her about his children? "Find somebody else to take care of your kid." On the way into the house and, more importantly, her bedroom, she glanced over her shoulder. "Maybe Katlin or Grace will be willing to help you. I don't have time for either you or your kid."

"No worries, man. Mama will help us." Until Santiago had spoken, Nita hadn't even realized the housekeeper's son was standing next to Daniel. She had to do a double-take when the Costa Rican native lifted a small blond boy onto his hip. Even from thirty feet away, she couldn't mistake the child's distinct Callahan eyes.

Fucking men.

"Uncle Ti, my tummy hurt." The small voice was like a giant hand that scooped up the shards of Nita's heart and ground it to dust.

She didn't need this shit in her life. She didn't need children...or a man. Especially Daniel Callahan. Her brain was simply too tired to analyze why the fact that he had kids upset her. What she needed was undisturbed sleep.

Nita walked quietly into the house so as not to wake her teammates and straight to her room.

But sleep wouldn't come.

Voices drifted up from the large common area. She rolled to her side pulling an extra pillow over her ears.

More than once she heard her name mentioned. Her team knew of her aversion to dealing with children although they hadn't a clue why. They were also very protective of her time and familiar with the long hours she'd been keeping in the clean room.

They hadn't been idle, either. They'd been called out twice to evacuate Americans from the U.S. Embassy. Thanks to the cool new helicopter flown by Black Swan team two, they were able to deliver the evacuees to the fleet in the Pacific Ocean then return with equipment for the new lab.

Nita rolled over again and gave up on sleep. The five women of Black Swan team two seemed nice enough, but she'd been so busy she hadn't even had time to get to know any of them. She did know that one was a nurse, or maybe she was a nurse practitioner. The one with short spiky hair if she remembered right.

Maybe she was downstairs taking care of Daniel's kids. Or perhaps Rosita had taken on those duties. She'd raised three boys and two girls in addition to running the Callahan compound for over twenty-five years. Nita was sure the outstanding cook and housekeeper could handle a sick baby.

The last thing Nita remembered before exhaustion forced her body—and thankfully her mind—to sleep, was multiple footsteps coming up the dual staircases to the suites on the second floor.

Bright daylight and a warm ocean breeze streamed through the screen. She'd forgotten to close the door the night before, along with the blackout drapes. Glancing at her colorful watch with its purple band, a personal protest against the completely white clean room garb, Nita realized she'd actually achieved her goal of six hours sleep. Now she needed coffee and some of Rosita's excellent breakfast before she returned to the space-like suit and recycled air of the clean room. Hopefully after today they wouldn't need her extra pair of hands, and she could return to her duties as one of the Ladies of Black Swan.

She much preferred being Lieutenant Banks to Dr. Banks. Bullets were better than Bunsen burners any day of the week. Knowing she'd have to shower before entering the vestibule to the clean room, Nita bypassed the one in her room and headed straight downstairs for coffee when she realized she'd never changed out of the scrubs she'd put on last night. Oh, well. She was dressed, even though she'd slept in those clothes.

As she wandered into the large dining room, her mouth watered at the smell of the breakfast on the buffet. She grabbed a plate and started down the line. Behind her, several members of Black Swan team two chatted with Lei Lu and Tori. She noticed Daniel sat at the far end beside his sister with an empty seat between him and Santiago.

A crash near the small table where coffee and juice was dispensed grabbed Nita's attention. The small boy, obviously only two or three, had dropped his juice. The glass shattered on the tile floor. Immediately, Nita set her almost full plate down and strode the five feet to the child.

"I *thorry*." He panted as his whole body began to shake. "I *thorry*, Aunt Katlin." He struggled but managed to pull off his T-shirt. Dropping to his knees, he used the cloth to wipe the floor of spilled juice.

Nita reached him first and placed a reassuring hand on his back. "It's okay." She hoped her voice was reassuring as she rubbed her hand up and down the child's back. Her sensitive fingers glided over bumps rather than smooth skin. She immediately tore her gaze from the mess on the floor to stare at his back. Her mouth dropped as she surveyed the multiple scars of varying lengths. Some were white and well-healed while others look less than a week old.

Daniel kneeled in front of them with the cloth napkins from the table. "It's okay, Simon."

Katlin dropped to her knees next to her brother and started picking up glass shards.

"Who the fuck did this to him?" Nita seethed as she glared at Daniel.

Katlin gasped. She pulled the boy into her lap. "Who hurt you, sweetheart?"

The boy began to shake his head violently. "I bad. I *thorry* I *pill* juice. Won't do it again. I *thorry,*" he gasped out between panicked pants.

She pulled her nephew to her chest and rocked him. "You are not a bad boy. Accidents happen." She rubbed up and down his scarred back. "You are a good boy, and no one will ever hurt you again."

Both women stared at Daniel.

Nita leaned forward until her face was inches from his. "Who the fuck tortured that little boy? Was it you?"

"What the fuck are you talking about?" Daniel looked past her to his son shaking in Katlin's arms.

His sister glared at him. "How could you let anyone do this to him?"

"Do what?" Daniel actually had the gall to sound confused.

"Are you fucking blind?" Nita pointed at his son. "Look at that child's back."

Daniel leaned over and stared in shock. With shaking hands, he reached for his son. The boy immediately moved to his father, favoring his left arm. "Daddy. I *thorry*. I didn't mean *pill juith.*"

"Son, I don't care about the juice. I care about you." Daniel carefully lifted the small face to his. "Who hurt you? Who did this to your back?"

Simon's entire body shivered in reaction. "No. Can't tell. I bad."

CHAPTER 8

Nita's outrage was only tempered by the streaks running down Katlin's alabaster cheeks. This small child had brought the toughest woman she knew to tears.

From a few feet away, she examined the scars. A belt, maybe. All were straight lines.

Tori joined her teammates carrying a broom and dustpan to clean the nearly forgotten broken juice glass. "I'll take care of this. You take care of the boy."

"Bring him over to the light." Nita strode to the window, expecting Daniel to follow her orders. "Move your hands up some so I can see."

"No," Daniel insisted. He held Simon so they could both see the child's back. "Jesus Christ," he said just above a whisper. "What caused that?"

Nita lightly ran fingers over scars already white with age and barely touched one that looked almost new. The bruising underneath had just started to turn purple. The only other time she'd seen scarring like that had been on an abused teenager after his father, suffering from PTSD, had whipped the shit out of him with a leather belt.

"Daniel, are you telling me you've never seen these before?" She watched his face looking for the lie.

"No. Never." He glanced away from her intense gaze. "Their mother takes care of them. I haven't...my job..." He swallowed hard then returned his gaze to hers. "I should've been around more. I suck as a father."

Nita saw the truth in every word, as well as the unspoken embarrassment.

He shook his head. "I thought his mother was being protective, or considerate of my busy schedule, when she wouldn't let me give him his bath or change his diaper. That fucking bitch."

"Do you think your wife was protecting someone else? The real abuser?" Nita wanted to offer an alternative. No one wants to believe that their spouse could harm their children in such a horrific way, if in fact he was married. "Is a possible someone else was hurting your son?"

The astonishment on Daniel's face turned to anger. "First of all, I'm not married. Never have been and would certainly never marry their mother. She was a lying, cheating, conniving bitch. The only reason I hooked up with her was for the mission. She is...I mean *was*...Cristobal Maximo's sister."

"Whoa, wait one," Katlin interrupted. "You said she was, as in past tense." She glanced up at the small child in Daniel's large hands. Just above a whisper, she asked, "Did you kill her?"

"I didn't have to. The influenza did it for me." He shook his head. "And it was painful. This virus acts almost like dengue hemorrhagic fever, except worse."

"What the hell you saying?" Nita couldn't imagine anything that was more painful than dengue. On the other hand, maybe it wasn't the flu at all. She thought about the broken vials in the clean room in the basement of the presidential residence that had become an unprotected area after the EMP. If the Reston Ebola had been transmitted in the air, they could have an epidemic on their hands.

"Daddy, I be down now?" Simon's small voice broke Nita's train of thought.

"Sure, son." The child winced as Daniel turned him around and set him in the chair next to Santiago. "Will you keep an eye on him, please?"

"Sure, I got the little guy." The handsome Latino smiled down at the child as he ruffled his uncombed blond hair.

Daniel returned to where Katlin and Nita still stood.

"Explain why you think it's like dengue?" Nita insisted.

He glanced at the table as though reassuring himself his son was taken care of, then refocused on Nita. "When it first starts, it comes across just like the regular flu with a high fever. Many of the people in camp experienced a severe headache and muscle pain, but there again, the flu can give you those symptoms as well. Then there's vomiting and diarrhea, often accompanied by horrendous abdominal pain. But I've never seen the flu cause bleeding the way this one does. Just carrying this old woman to the infirmary caused bruising behind her knees and across her shoulders. It's the strangest thing I've ever seen. The slightest scrape will bleed for hours, like it does with dengue."

"Did the patients get a rash? Or clumps of little red spots like with dengue?" Nita needed to pin down as many facts as possible.

Daniel seemed to think long and hard before he answered. "No. I don't remember anybody getting the spots."

"What about a sore throat?" Nita pressed. That was another symptom of the well-known, subtropical virus.

This time Daniel didn't hesitate. "No. The doctor in camp

was looking for that complaint, and no one seemed to have that symptom. He mentioned that the hemorrhaging was so much worse than with dengue. It was as though the body just started shutting down, bleeding both internally and externally."

Oh, fuck! With every symptom Daniel described, Nita was more convinced it was Ebola, not some super strength influenza. "Who were the first to get sick?"

"I'm not one hundred percent sure, but I think it was my men from the EMP mission. They were sick within about twenty-four hours."

Relentlessly, she asked the next question, fearing its answer. "Has anybody died in the camp?"

"Yes." Daniel seemed to gather himself before he continued. "Some of my best and strongest men. The way they died..." He shook his head. "These were warriors, and they died with no dignity left...bodily fluids practically poured out of them." He glanced up the stairway. "I had to get my kids out of there."

"What are you thinking?" Katlin sounded anxious.

Nita ignored her question and glanced around the dining room and living room. All the Ladies of Black Swan, both teams, had received the inoculations of the CDC serum. So had Daniel. Her gaze fell on Santiago animatedly entertaining Simon. She looked to her team leader. "Did Santiago get the shot?" She didn't need to explain what shot.

Katlin nodded. "Yes. So did everyone on the household staff." Her eyes grew wide. After working together for so many years, they could practically read each other's thoughts. "Do you really think it—"

"Don't say it," Nita warned her team leader. "Daniel, just give me an estimate, how many in your camp are dead?"

He shrugged. "When I left, two hundred, maybe two fifty.

That's about twenty-five percent. More than half the camp was sick."

Nita nodded. "So some are surviving?"

"Yeah, some of my men seemed to be getting better when we left." Then he noted, "The children were only mildly affected, but several months ago they had gotten flu shots sent to us by the CDC."

Nita wondered if the inoculations were a means of human testing outside the United States. Even though the Reston Ebola had first been discovered more than one hundred miles away, she was thankful that the children in Daniel's camp had been given the shots.

"Was the baby given the shot?" She wasn't even sure how old the child was. She racked her brain to try to remember at what ages children receive the standard shots.

Daniel's lips drew into a thin line. "Bella wasn't born yet, and her mother refused the shot fearing it would harm the child."

"She should've gotten the shot. It may have saved her life and your daughter's." As soon as the words were out of Nita's mouth she kicked her own ass. Damn. She needed a filter. Trying to cover for her mistake, she added, "Mothers pass antibodies on to their infants. It's nature's way of protecting innocent babies."

"Is it wrong for me not to feel bad that their mother is dead?" Katlin asked nobody in particular.

"If that bitch wasn't already dead, I'd go back and kill her myself, right now," Daniel seethed.

Embarrassed to ask, but as the only doctor, she needed to know. "How's the baby doing?"

Daniel's jaw sawed back and forth before he spoke through gritted teeth. "Better, no thanks to you."

"Kira is tending to her." Katlin glared at her brother. "Her last rotation as a nurse practitioner was in pediatrics. She was really good at finding those tiny veins and getting liquids into my beautiful little niece. I checked on her just before coming down for breakfast. She seems to be doing much better today."

"She thinks Bella's fever finally broke a few hours ago," Daniel announced. "Kira got the right combination of meds into her. At least she's resting peacefully now."

"Is Kira the one with spiky blonde hair or is she the brunette with big Bambi eyes?" Damn, Nita really did need to get to know the Ladies of Black Swan team two. But there hadn't been time. They had stayed at the hotel rather than the Callahan compound so the little free time she'd had in the last few days, she hadn't run into them, until she'd come down for breakfast this morning.

"She has the short blond hair." Katlin smiled. "I don't think it's supposed to stick up in the air like it did the other night. I believe that was caused by her helmet."

Well, that made sense. In Nita's mind though, she would always be the spiky blonde. She looked longingly at her plate of food that was growing colder by the moment. "I need to eat and get back over to the lab."

They all sat down to finish the meal. Nita noticed that Simon favored his left arm. From several chairs away, it looked slightly swollen and definitely black and blue. That could mean that he was coming down with Ebola—which she suspected was the true virus that had infected the guerrilla camp—or the boy was hiding even more injuries. She hadn't forgotten about the multiple scars that would mar his back for life.

Throughout the meal, Nita hadn't dared to look at Daniel. She knew what she'd see. Condemnation and despise. He had every right to feel that way. She hadn't been able to help him or his child last night.

As soon as she was finished eating, Nita walked around to Simon's seat and kneeled to be eye level with the child. "Hi there, Simon. I'm Nita." She purposely held out her hand to shake his. He reached his right hand out, careful of his left arm tucked in at the waist. After a brief shake, she asked, "Does your arm hurt?"

His gaze rose to meet his father's. Daniel chewed for a second, swallowed, then instructed, "Answer the doctor's question."

"You a doctor?" Simon's eyes were so big she could see the white completely surrounding the beautiful light and dark blues.

Nita couldn't help but smile at the child's surprise. "Yes, I am. But I have to make a confession, I'm not very good with kids. I usually only work on adults."

She felt Daniel's eyes bore into her, but she didn't dare look up.

With her gaze locked on Simon's, Nita asked, "May I touch your arm?"

The boy twisted away from her, clamping his left arm tightly to his body.

"Simon, let Nita look at your arm," his father commanded.

The child looked up at Daniel from under long blond lashes. "Mama *thay* no doctor. I no go to doctor. Not allowed."

Daniel's jaw worked side-to-side before he spoke. "You're with me now, and we go to the doctor. Let Nita take a look at your arm."

After a long moment, the boy swung his legs around the side of the chair giving Nita better access.

His left arm was considerably larger than the right. The swelling was made evident by the fact that he was a little on the skinny side. A glance up at Katlin was all she needed. Her friend headed to the medical bag the team carried. Within thirty seconds, she was back with what looked like a standard tablet. It wasn't. She held one of the most high-tech x-ray machines on the planet next to the child's bicep.

"Fuck." The word escaped on a huffed breath.

Simon smiled at her. "Me see fuck?"

What the hell? "I'm sorry, Simon. What did you say?"

The child pointed to his bicep. "Fuck. You taked a picture of my fuck." He pointed to the tablet. "Can I see picture of my fuck?"

Nita wanted to crawl in a hole and die. Where the hell was that filter? Another reason she didn't like being around children, they heard and repeated everything like human parrots. As long as she was around Daniel's children, she would have to be more aware of her language.

Santiago bent back in his chair so he could see her. Grinning from ear-to-ear, he goaded her. "Come on, Nita, show Simon his fuck."

With the fingers hidden under the tablet, she raised the middle one toward the very good-looking, but hard-edged man. "Oh, I found the fuck for you, too, Santiago."

"Enough. You're teaching my nephew bad words," Katlin chastised, unable to hide the smile. She bent down so her face was even with Simon's. "Has anyone taught you about adult words?"

The child shook his head "No, Aunt Katlin."

"There are certain words only adults can say," she explained. "Fuck is one of those words."

"Around this house, the poor kid is going to hear more adult words than kid words," Tori noted.

"Wait till he meets Damnit." Lei Lu reminded everyone of the hundred-pound puppy they shared. "He'll get totally confused."

"Nita, what did you see?" Daniel's quiet voice cut through the adult banter.

She had actually taken an x-ray. To divert attention away from any more discussion of swearwords, Nita pointed as she explained, "Simon, this is your bicep and there is a bone that runs all the way from your shoulder to your elbow."

"Is it hurt?" the boy asked.

"Not this time," she blurted out.

Daniel's glare shot spears at her.

Why the hell couldn't she keep her big mouth shut and stick to the facts?

She pasted on a small smile. "See these bumps on your bone?" When the boy nodded she continued. "This is where your bone was broken before and has healed."

Katlin, who had been leaning over Nita shoulder, sucked in an audible breath.

Undaunted, Nita pushed on. "The good news is I don't see any new breaks. Can I take a picture of this part of your arm?"

He gasped when she tried to flatten out the forearm. She quickly held the tablet and snapped an x-ray from elbow to fingers. Studying the shot, she grimaced.

"I want to see," Simon requested.

Nita glanced over her shoulder at Katlin then up to Daniel. Her friend had seen the problem, but Daniel hadn't realized what he was looking at. She turned the tablet to give him a better view.

Jagged black lines cut through white bone images in the radial and ulna. "We call this a greenstick fracture because it travels not just across the bone, but up." She looked into

Simon's pretty eyes, sparkling with tears. "Congratulations, you have a broken arm." Then she looked at Daniel and over to Santiago. "I'll bet you men had broken arms when you two were boys, didn't you?"

Daniel jumped on the opening. "When I was five, I fell out of a tree and broke my arm. Did you fall and break yours, too?"

"No." Simon's answer was a single syllable just above a whisper.

Santiago picked up on the questioning. "I was eight when I broke mine. Hurt like a mother f—...hel—...really bad. I got hit with a flying baseball bat. The boy in front of me had just hit the ball, and he threw the bat behind him so he could run to first base. I was walking up to the warm-up box. I tried to hit it away with my arm, but it broke right here." He pointed to a scar. "I had to go to the hospital and have an operation."

Huge eyes looked at Nita. "Operation? At *hothpital*?" The negative jerks of his head and the jiggling of his jaw made Nita reach out and pull the boy to her.

"No, no," she soothed. "No hospital or operation for you. I can fix it right here, but I might need a little help from your Aunt Katlin." It wouldn't be the first time Nita and Katlin had reset a bone a long way from the hospital. She started pulling out the necessary equipment.

Within half an hour, Simon's left arm was in a cast and snugged up in the sling. He was also the center of attention of every woman in the house.

When Nita stepped into the hall powder room to wash off her hands, Daniel filled the doorway. "A greenstick fracture is usually caused from the arm being twisted."

"That's true." She soaped her hands.

He hung his head. "Simon told me it happened last week,

before his mother got sick. They were walking to the nearby village, and he couldn't keep up with her so she twisted his arm and threatened him." He drew in a ragged breath. "Christ, Nita, I had no idea what she was doing to him." His jaw shifted back and forth before he clamped his teeth. In that moment, he looked so much like his son, so strong on the outside yet fiercely trying to control his emotions.

Instincts she didn't know she had, forced her to wrap her arms around her friend. "You have a lifetime to make it up to your son."

When his arms enveloped her, their closeness felt right. She'd been held by lots of other men, probably hundreds, but it had never felt like this. Maybe it was because they'd known each other for so long, and after hours of conversation the last time they'd been together, Daniel truly knew her. That changed their dynamic. She blanked her mind and concentrated on the way his body heat forced its way into her, warming her all the way to her soul.

"Thank you, Nita, for fixing my son's broken arm." Daniel gave her an extra squeeze. "I'm sorry for snapping at you earlier about Bella. Katlin tried to tell me last night that you don't like kids. You don't treat children. I didn't believe her. I just couldn't believe that you would walk away from any sick child, especially mine. I still don't understand, but I accept the fact that you don't like to treat children. That makes it all the more special that you worked on my son today."

He leaned back slightly then lifted her chin until their eyes met. He stared at her face for the longest moment. "You're lying to yourself, you know. You love children. I saw the fierce mama bear in you come out swinging, ready to take on anyone who would dare hurt a child. That wasn't just Dr. Banks gently wrapping my son's broken arm, that was a woman who cares deeply about kids. You can lie to everyone else, Nita, and you can even lie to yourself, but I see the woman you hide deep inside."

His warm lips touched hers for the briefest of kisses.

When she opened her eyes, he was gone.

CHAPTER 9

*W*OMEN ARE SO FUCKING CONFUSING. *I* JUST NEED TO STAY AWAY *from them.* Daniel reconsidered his thoughts for a moment then readjusted. *No. I like fucking women too much to stay away forever.* He enjoyed the games of tease and retreat. *It's my foreplay. They are sizing me up just as much as I am considering every physical aspect of them. They're making the decision whether to spend a few hours with me while I'm trying to decide how good they'd be in bed.*

But it wasn't like that with Nita. He slowly climbed the stairs to the second-floor suites. There were no games between them, although she was an expert at flirtation and a damn good judge of men. She'd played her scenes well when supposedly seducing him at the resort bar next door, allowing him to escape from the men in his Nicaraguan camp so he could sleep in his own bed in the Callahan compound.

But that one night, relaxed in the pillows of the couch in the house he considered his home, honesty had changed everything. He'd let his guard down with her. He hadn't even considered taking her to bed. That night, he hadn't needed sex to take the edge off the reality of his life. Like a master craftsman in a woodshop, using only her gritty subject matter, she had ground off his hard-pointed corners a micrometer at a time and left him smooth. Contented.

When they had both finally retreated to separate bedrooms, he'd found something he'd never discovered before...a female friend. One who truly cared for him. Nita didn't need him to make her life better like the whores in camp, nor did she seem to be impressed by his monetary value. They had simply been two tired people who worked inside a dark world, enjoying each other's company. He'd never had anything like that in his life with a woman.

After his parents had abandoned him to the care of his grandparents while they took his precious sister and moved to a different continent, Daniel had attended the local high school. At fourteen, though, all the adults in his life had agreed he should attend a military high school. He'd seen it as another way that his father had shirked his manly responsibilities onto someone else, in that case it was the headmaster and teachers at the residential school.

Surrounded by hundreds of other teenage boys, he never got the opportunity to become friends with a girl. Females were seen as objects of fantasy and for fucking. Adding to this distorted opinion, was the fact that Daniel didn't really have a sister. Although genetically Katlin was his sibling, they had only lived in the same household for three years. Sure, his parents would fly him to Costa Rica during school holidays where, for a week or two, they would pretend to be one big happy family, but in the end, he'd find himself back on that single cot in the stark dormitory rather than a comfortable home with his family.

Katlin had been the universe to his parents. From the moment Daniel had understood his mother was pregnant, the baby had become the most important thing in everyone's life.

At eight years old, he'd been afraid his mother was going to die when she'd been put on maternity bed rest. He feared the child inside her was going to kill her and he couldn't imagine life without his loving mother. As an adult, he understood that his mom had miscarried several babies, and needed to remain immobile in order to carry his sister to term. At some point in between, that childhood terror had transformed into resentment for his sister.

When Katlin had been born, all the attention bestowed upon him as the only child and grandchild of his generation had been refocused on her. Sure, all of his needs had been met. He never missed a hearty meal, always had clean clothes that properly fit, his parents still read him bedtime stories, and they all attended mass on Saturday night or Sunday morning. But his life had changed when his sister had been born.

He would never forget the Sunday afternoon when his parents announced that they were leaving the United States and Daniel would be left behind to live with his grandparents. Nor would he ever forgive his father.

As he reached the top of the long staircase, Daniel glanced at the double doors at the end of the hall that opened to his suite where Kira was taking care of his beautiful baby Bella.

It should be Nita in there. She's a doctor. He wanted the best care for his baby. He just didn't understand Nita's problem. Last night she'd said she couldn't deal with kids and practically threw his sick daughter back into his arms. Six hours later, she'd gently wrapped his son's broken arm and accused him of being a terrible father.

Simon's battered and scarred back filled Daniel's vision and forced him to stop halfway down the hall. Oh, fuck. He *was* a terrible father. He'd allowed that crazy bitch to harm his boy. He'd allowed himself to be so consumed by the job that he'd forgotten what was truly important in his life, his children.

He'd become his father.

Staring at the ornately carved Brazilian wood doors thirty feet away, Daniel vowed to become the father he never had. With determination, he strode into his rooms.

Last night they had moved furniture around in the living area to accommodate a crib, changing table and a rocker that Rosita had found for him. It wasn't an ideal nursery, but it was comfortable and separate from his bedroom. The pretty blonde rocked his six-month-old baby while giving her a bottle of red tinged liquid. "Did you eat?" Her tone was soft, but her silver blue eyes were accusing.

When the Army lieutenant had arrived to check on the IV an hour ago, he'd been exhausted from interrupted sleep on the couch. He'd never had to take care of Bella all by himself before so every time she moved, whimpered, sighed, he'd instantly come awake and dashed to the crib. "I had a good breakfast. There's still plenty down there." He reached for the precious bundle in her arms. "Go grab some food. It's mostly local fare, but the cook will whip you up an omelet or French toast if you'd like."

"My mouth is already watering. We were on board the aircraft carrier for over two weeks eating cafeteria-style food. Trust me; a home-cooked meal sounds great." Kira gracefully rose. "Sit. I'll hand her to you. She's not quite finished with this bottle."

Daniel did as directed. "What's in there?"

She deftly dodged the plastic tubing running into Bella's arm as she transferred the baby to him. "Rosita made it. Her Spanish dialect is little different from what I learned in language school, but from what I could understand, it's water infused with several fruits. What she really needs is electrolytes made specifically for babies."

"I'll get some sent in on the next shipment." He closed his eyes dreading that phone call. Uncle Tom, in family mode, would be thrilled about becoming a great uncle. The man, who had been more of a father to him than his own, would treat Simon and Isabella like grandchildren. They were going to be spoiled rotten once they all return to the United States.

Tom Gilpatrick, though, would be pissed as hell that one of his agents had created not one, but two children, while working undercover in a Third World country. It wasn't Daniel's fault, though. Both pregnancies were caused by busted condoms provided by the crazy bitch. More than once he'd wondered if she'd somehow weakened the latex or poked a hole in it on purpose. He'd never had unprotected sex. Never. There's too much bad shit out there in the world, and he had no desire to die from fucking.

When he opened his eyes, Kira was injecting something into the IV. "She'll probably sleep for a couple hours. I thought we had her fever under control, but it is still jumping up and down. The acetaminophen seems to be helping." She smiled at him over her shoulder. "I like seeing a father take care of his baby." After disposing of the needle, she said, "I think I'll take you up on that breakfast. I'm sure the hotel has already finished serving. I'll come back up and check on her before I leave."

Daniel stared down at the small life he held. Tiny hands pretended to hold the bottle as she sucked away, bliss written in her miniature features. She was as helpless as he felt. What the hell did he know about raising kids? Sure, he'd been around Katlin when she was a baby, or at least the first four years. He had definitive memories about stinky diapers, but remembered laughing at the disgusted face she'd made when he'd fed her peas for the very first time. Those were followed by happier memories.

He and Santiago had teased Katlin to the point of tears when they were in their early teens. By the time she'd reached that same age, she'd already killed several men, defending children the ages of his during an attempted coup.

Bella's angelic face told him nothing of her future. Would she be the fierce warrior that her Aunt Katlin was today? Or would she be the refined woman hosting parties for princes and ambassadors like his mother? Or would she be fucking crazy like the woman who gave birth to her? Only time would tell.

With a sigh, his daughter released the nipple she'd been sucking. Her head rolled to the side. He threw the small towel over his shoulder then placed his baby's head next to his cheek. He'd just learned the skills last night from Rosita along with the lesson that babies had to be burped after feeding. He gently patted her back until she belched like a frat boy. For some reason he couldn't explain, that made him proud.

After laying her back in the crib and tucking her in, Daniel drew in a deep breath and reached for his phone. Rather than calling him through normal contacts, he dialed his uncle's private cell phone.

"Daniel, are you all right?" The fatherly concern on the other end touched Daniel in a way he could never explain, nor wanted to.

"Hey, Uncle Tom, I need to talk to you about something very personal." A fist tightened in his gut. Daniel was embarrassed that he hadn't proudly called his uncle and announced the birth of his son three years ago. He'd wonder why later, but right now he needed to get on with it.

"You know, son, you can talk to me about anything." Tom

often called anyone younger than him, son, but that term of endearment suddenly meant more to Daniel than he'd ever imagined.

"Look, uhm, I'm just going to come right out and say this... I need your help to get my son and daughter into the United States without hassles." Daniel took a deep breath as he waited for the explosion on the other end of the line.

There was no sound whatsoever for a long time. Daniel pulled the phone away from his ear and looked at it to see that they were still connected. "Uncle Tom?"

He heard a long inhalation of breath. "There are so many things wrong with that statement, I don't know where to start." On a heavy exhale, he began, "First, are you sure the children are yours."

"Definitely. They have my eyes, the only blue ones in camp." From the moment those children were born, he'd never doubted their parentage. Those unique Irish eyes, the ones that matched the man on the other end of the phone, were as much proof as any DNA test.

"Very well." Keys clicking could be heard to the line. "I don't suppose they have birth certificates?"

At that, Daniel laughed. "The previous president of Nicaragua wasn't big on birth certificates or death certificates, so that answer would be, no."

"Hmm. That could play to our advantage," Tom noted. "How do you feel about your children carrying dual citizenship with Costa Rica?"

"That's one hell of an idea." Daniel smiled. Not everyone in the Costa Rican government liked the fact that of four U.S. government employees owned a large resort hotel, a private compound, a private airstrip, and nearly a hundred acres of prime real estate on the Caribbean coast. He glanced at his daughter sleeping peacefully. She and Simon, as Costa Rican citizens, could own his share, skirting around any legislation they imposed.

"We may need to grease some more palms around Barra del Colorado, but I'm sure the local officials would be more than happy to help us. We've proven to be a true boost to their economy." Neither Tom Gilpatrick nor Daniel Callahan were averse to bribes. They were very familiar with the fact that in most Third World countries, American dollars could buy you almost anything, including certified birth certificates and passports.

"Works for me," Daniel agreed. "I'll handle that this afternoon."

"Daniel, what of their mother?" Tom chuckled. "Or mothers?"

"Singular. And that fucking bitch is dead." It took everything within Daniel to hold back the fury he had for the woman who had given birth to his children, then abused his son.

"Did you kill her?" Tom asked as though he were referring to his breakfast.

"Didn't have to. The flu, which may have really been Ebola, killed her two days ago." Daniel needed to shift gears and put on his CIA hat.

"What's the status back in the camp?"

"When I left, the farmers and townspeople were bringing their sick and dying to our doc, but he didn't have anywhere near enough supplies to handle them." He had to ask. "Is there any chance I could get a shipment of pain medication, rehydration packs, or anything else physicians in the states give patients who have the flu?"

"You have a resupply plane coming in a few hours for the scientists. I've included a few cases of those medicines, but nowhere near enough for the guerilla camp. I sent those to

Costa Rica just in case anybody there got sick, although if Nita has done her job, all our people should have been inoculated." Under his breath Tom added, "I just hope that shit works."

"It has so far," Daniel reassured his uncle. "I must have had a dose of Ebola though, because I ended up sleeping on and off for almost three days. When I woke up, I felt great." He sat on the edge of his bed and glanced into the crib. "Bella, that's what we call her, got hit pretty hard. Do you think on the next shipment down here you could send me some electrolytes and aspirin made specifically for babies? Simon, my son—"

"His name is Simon?" Tom interrupted in a choked voice.

Daniel smiled. "Yes, I gave him Grandpa Gilpatrick's name." It was also his uncle's middle name, one that had been given to the oldest boy in every generation for over a hundred years.

"Thank you for that, son." Tom audibly swallowed hard.

"It was the right thing to do," Daniel admitted. Needing to change the subject, and wanting to get this part out there, he asked, "How soon can I be brought in? I want to get my kids the hell out of here. I want them to grow up in the U.S."

"Understood, but we really need you there for now. Was Cristobal Maximo still alive when you left camp?"

"Yes, and doing well. The shots you sent about six months ago were used on the children, the pregnant, and the important which included Cris." Well, not all the pregnant women took the shots. Damn her. Daniel had made sure they stretched the solution as far as it could possibly go.

"Did you take the shot?" Tom's direct question hit the spot.

"No, sir, not then. I wanted to make sure everyone was protected against the flu, but there wasn't enough to go around." Even giving children partial doses, there had barely been enough to include the doctor, who was essential, and Cris. Emilio had also deemed himself important and taken a full dose. "We had already started recruiting for the coup and the numbers in camp were in the hundreds. But Nita gave me the shot when I first saw her."

"You do know that wasn't the flu shot, right? It was the first batch of serum against the Ebola found in northeastern Nicaragua last year that was ready for human testing. I sent it to you because I wanted you and your camp protected."

"Thank you for that. There simply wasn't enough," Daniel insisted.

"And being the conscientious leader that you are, you wanted to make sure everyone else was served first." Once again Tom was accurate.

Daniel had always been taught to make sure his troops were housed and fed before he was. It was a leadership style he'd learned while training with the Marines. *Treat your men right, and they'll follow you into hell...and out the other side in victory.* The mantra had been repeated so many times, and demonstrated constantly by the officers in charge that taking care of everyone else first had become an unconscious decision for him.

Trying to force the conversation back around to his children leaving Central America, he asked, "You mentioned that you needed me here. Is there something specific you need me to do before I leave?"

"Yes. We're getting mixed reports out of Nicaragua. The new official government is requesting international aid due to the overwhelming flu epidemic. If what you just told me is true, that this is really the Ebola strain discovered nearly a year ago, they are in more trouble than they know. Other agents are reporting thousands dead. Our man on the streets

in Managua said it looks like a zombie apocalypse movie
with dead bloated bodies just tossed into the streets."

Daniel could only imagine how terrible it must be inside a
city with no electricity, in the heat and humidity of summer.

"As you well know, we have the best satellites in the
world, but they can't give us the human intelligence we need
to make good decisions. I'm ordering you to Managua. I want
you to pick up our asset there then check out the situation in
San Miguelito."

Tom finally took a breath before he continued. "Satellite
pictures coming in show absolutely no progress on the new
capital. The United States needs General Cortez's new
government to stand up quickly and to start digging that
damn canal. We're willing to send them anything they need in
order to keep that government friendly toward the U.S.A."

"Will do," Daniel promised. "What you want me to do
with the Managua asset?"

"Leave him in San Miguelito. Set him up with you as his
new handler."

"Yes, sir." Daniel hoped the disappointment didn't come
through in his voice. This was his job and it wasn't done until
Deputy Director Thomas Gilpatrick told him to come home.

"Hey, Daniel," Tom's voice had changed to the gentle one
he'd used so often while Daniel was a teen and in college.
"Congratulations on the children. Could you do me a favor?
Use that secure phone in your hand and take pictures of
Simon and Bella. Send them to me right away."

"For the passports?" Daniel speculated.

"Fuck, no. I'm going to frame them and put them on my
desk." There was a short pause before he added, "And the
handler assignment, it's just temporary. DD CIA out."

Daniel closed the connection on his end and opened the
camera app. As he was moving around Bella's crib for the

best shot, one that didn't include the needle in her arm or the tubing, a soft knock came at the door.

"Daniel," Katlin whispered. "We have orders to fly you into Nicaragua."

He zoomed in on the tiny face with light pink cheeks. As though his daughter knew exactly what he needed, she opened those beautiful blue eyes and smiled up at him.

Click. Click. Click.

Grace stepped next to Daniel. "Oh, goody. She's awake. I love babies." She picked up the child and started with nonstop baby talk. "Are we going to have fun together while Daddy is off working? You bet we are, baby Bella. We're going to read a book. We're going to get a bottle when we need one." She lifted the child and sniffed loudly. "But right this minute, we're going to get a fresh new diaper." She looked at Daniel. "In case you hadn't figured it out, I'm going to take care of the baby since Kira is on the chopper crew."

"Where's Simon?" Daniel kicked off the flip-flops he'd worn to breakfast and grabbed a pair of black socks from the drawer and his boots. "I need to take a picture of him and send it to Uncle Tom before we go."

"You'd better send a copy of those same pictures to Uncle Francis, too. You know how competitive those two are when it comes to you and me. Can you imagine how bad they're going to be about the kids? It will be a constant competition about who can buy the biggest and best presents."

His sister was right. He needed to send the same pictures to both uncles. Why did families have to be so fucking complicated?

CHAPTER 10

DAMN MEN. WHO NEEDS THEM ANYWAY?

Nita stomped on the abrasive rug to remove as much sand from her flip-flops and body as possible before entering the vestibule. She hit the large metal panel that opened the first set of doors. Stepping through, they rapidly closed behind her as the first line of prevention to keep germs out.

I certainly don't need Daniel Callahan. I could walk in that resort bar right this minute and have any man I want begging to take me upstairs to his room within an hour.

Taking tiny steps across the sticky mat she attempted to remove as many fine particles as possible. She walked to a locker designated as hers and slipped out of her clothes and into a new paper robe before entering the wet shower. After scrubbing every inch of her body with antiseptic soap, she rinsed off with treated water and stepped into a drying tube under ultraviolet-C lights that reached down to DNA to kill viruses, yet posed no known threats to humans.

Too bad the shower and lights couldn't wash away her anger. She'd had the whole walk from the Callahan compound to the new clean room to think about what had happened. She would never be able to erase the picture in her mind of little Simon's scarred back and multiple fractures.

How could Daniel have let this happen to his child? Any child, but especially his. Sure, he claims he didn't know, but how could he not? Was he that much of an asshole to be a totally absent father? Little more than a sperm donor? And how could he have kept two children a secret from his entire family, especially Katlin?

Nita just didn't understand.

With practiced hands, she grabbed a new jumpsuit from the shelf and slipped into it, flipping up the hood to cover her hair. Next came the latex gloves and her personal crocs. She didn't need to think about the clean room protocol. Good thing. Her mind was filled with Daniel.

He had kissed her, right there in the bathroom. And he'd apologized. That was the Daniel Callahan she thought she knew.

Balancing on one foot at a time, she slipped booties over her shoes then walked through the plastic curtain into the next phase of dressing.

Anger rose again when she considered what she'd found when she'd gone upstairs to check on the baby...he'd been flirting with Kira. Or at least that's what it sounded like through the closed doors. Nita wasn't about to walk in and see for herself. She had better things to do than deal with a baby.

At least that was the lie she told herself. Even she didn't believe it.

She lifted the heavy helmet with her name on it and checked the clear face shield. Everything looked fine. Carefully placing it over her head, she wiggled her shoulders for a more comfortable fit. Next came the thick coveralls that looked like a damn spacesuit. It took a little maneuvering to get a tight, smooth fit, but she managed.

As she stepped into the boots, Daniel's words sliced through her.

He was right.

She was lying to herself. And had been for years.

Nita couldn't walk into that bedroom and see clear liquids running through a tube from a hanging bag into an arm that was strapped to a board. At least there were no beeping machines. Although, Nita had noticed that the pulse-ox apparatus was missing from her medical equipment bag.

As a physician, she had an obligation to check on the patient. She'd been frozen in place. She couldn't force herself to close the short distance to Daniel's door.

There was a tiny baby inside that was sick...and might die. Nita couldn't have the death of another child on her conscience. The last one had ruined a promising career and sent Nita into an emotional depth she never wanted to see again. She'd gone on a ten-day drunk, fucked men she would never remember, missed her medical school final exams, and ended up in the emergency room with an alcohol overdose.

Fortunately, the Uniformed Services Medical School board had allowed her to graduate based on her stellar classroom scores and physician observations. They'd allowed her to become a doctor. But, she had lost her residency.

She needed to get out of Washington, D.C. as fast as possible, and as far away from the neonatal unit as she could get.

As a newly promoted Army captain, the military didn't have any problem sending her half a world away to deal with emergency medicine in Iraq. Nita had recovered her sanity and found her purpose amidst the blood and guts and gore close to the front line. She'd also discovered the endorphins created by working out hard. When she wasn't in the makeshift medical center, she could often be found pumping iron with the men in Special Forces or running in full gear and a heavy pack.

Compared to what she'd put herself through in the Middle Eastern desert, the Joint All-Female Special Operations School was easy. So was the subsequent SEAL, Special Forces, and Marine SpecOps training. She'd loved every minute of it.

Nita had always loved the thrill and breakneck pace of the emergency room but didn't understand that she was an adrenaline junkie until she'd completed JAFSOS. It was how she dealt with life when she didn't want to deal with life.

She backed up to the self-contained breathing apparatus and shrugged into the shoulder straps. Hopefully, they would have the specialized air system set soon so all she had to do was plug into one of the tubes in the clean room. But until then, everyone working on Ebola had to carry their own fresh and recycled air.

Facing the final door, she was ready to throw her mind into her work and shoved Daniel Callahan into a box and lock it. At least for a little while.

Six hours later, Nita was cross-eyed from looking at slides under the microscope. Nothing seemed to be killing this fucking virus. She stretched her back.

Chyna with a y brought over another drawer of vials and set them down on the metal table. Instead of leaving, though, she leaned against the edge and folded her hands in front of her settling in for a talk.

Fucking great. The intern's posture didn't speak of a scientific discussion.

"What can I do for you, Chyna?" Nita was never one to beat around the bush, nor did she feel like exchanging niceties. She felt hungry. If stripping out of this clean suit wasn't such a pain in the ass, Nita would seriously consider lunch.

"Can I ask you a question?"

"Do I have a choice?" Nita volleyed back.

Chyna simply smiled and pushed on. "Have you and Daniel been together long?"

"We're not together." Damn it. "His sister is one of my best friends and my team leader. I've known Daniel for years." Nita had only met Katlin's older brother two years earlier, but she made it sound longer on purpose.

"Oh." Chyna smiled. "So, you are just friends? Back in Managua, in the clean room, you seemed...very friendly."

Nita refused to answer. "Are these the last of the slides for today?" There was no way in hell she was going to discuss the kiss Daniel had given her that night.

As though surprised, Chyna looked down at the tray. It was her turn to ignore the question. "Since that was just a friendly kiss, that means Daniel is free and available?"

"I wouldn't know what his current status is." Then she told Chyna the truth, at least one version of it. "He just lost the mother of his children to this virus, and their baby girl is fighting for her life next-door. Fortunately, their son isn't showing symptoms yet."

Excitement oozed through Chyna's suit. "Daniel is here? Is he staying at the hotel?"

Nita rolled her eyes. Out of everything she'd just said, Chyna's take away was that Daniel was nearby. What a twit.

"No, he is not at the hotel." Nita hesitated for just a moment then decided to make things clear to the young student. "Daniel lives in the compound next door where we all stay every time we come to Costa Rica. He brought his three-year-old son and sick baby to me." Guilt washed over her because she was not the one who had cared for his child all night. Kira had taken on that duty. There was no reason to tell Chyna those facts.

"Is he still over there?" Chyna looked in that direction as though she could see the compound through the double-walled windowless clean room. "Does he come over to the hotel dining room to eat?"

"No. He doesn't take meals at the hotel. We have an excellent cook staff at the compound." Nita's tolerance of this questioning was about at an end. How dense could this girl be? She looked at the fresh innocent face inside the shield. "How old are you?"

"Twenty-five," she proudly announced.

"You have any idea how old Daniel is?" Nita had to take a mental step back and do some math. Katlin had just turned thirty and Daniel was eight years older. "He's thirteen years older than you."

"I like...prefer older men." Pink tinged the younger woman's cheeks. "They know what they're doing..." She glanced around the room, leaned in closer, and said just above a whisper, "In bed, you know."

Oh, Nita was well aware of the expertise older men brought to sex. She also knew how well inexperienced men took orders. She'd enjoyed more than her share of both. She wondered what sex with Daniel would be like. If the way he'd kissed her in the bathroom that morning was any indication, he'd be slow and gentle, tender and caring, assuring that she came first. Maybe he'd give her multiple orgasms before he slid into her. He was in great shape. He'd probably be able to go several times in the span of the night. Would he go balls to the wall, literally, taking her against a wall, a door? How about doggy style? She didn't mind helping out with her fingers if the man wasn't adept enough to reach around and work her clit. Then there was her favorite—

"Do you think Daniel would come over to the hotel if I invited him to have supper with me?" Chyna was certainly persistent. "I could offer him room service."

"You know what, Chyna, all this talk of food has made me hungry." Nita rose from the stool. "Sit here. Why don't you check this tray of slides and report your findings back to Dr. Johnson? I think I'm going to go next door and get some lunch, and then I'll check on Daniel's sick baby daughter." She slowly enunciated the last three words hoping the ditz would buy a clue.

An hour later, Nita shoved back from the dining room table after consuming her second bowl of fish and vegetable stew. Damn, Rosita could cook.

"So where is everyone?" she asked her teammate.

Tori ran a laundry list of everyone who went on the helicopter flight to Managua and San Miguelito. Nita was a little pissed that she hadn't gotten the opportunity to even ride in the Black Swan team two experimental helicopter, say nothing about fly it, yet Katlin was sitting second seat today. "Grace is upstairs babysitting. Lei Lu and Santiago took Simon for a ride in the jet boat, but they should be back any minute."

She had no sooner gotten the words out of her mouth and the front door blew open. Forty pounds of whirlwind ran toward her.

"*Mith* Nita. I *thaw* a turtle *thith* big." Simon tried to throw his arms wide, but the sling and cast only let one side work properly. Then, to her amazement, the child flung his good arm around her and crawled up into her lap. "Want to go *thee* the turtle?" His expression changed to one of complete seriousness. "You know how to drive a boat?"

Bursting out laughing, she wrapped her arms around the child and gave him a gentle hug. She couldn't help herself. She liked this kid. "Yes, Simon. I know how to drive the boat, but perhaps we should save that for another day. Did you have lunch?"

Santiago lifted the picnic basket as he walked by the dining table toward the kitchen. "That boy must have a hollow leg given how much food he ate. Thank Christ Mom packed a lot."

Rosita shot out of the kitchen. "I raised three boys, not counting Daniel. I know how much food kids eat." She patted her son's face. "Especially big boys."

He leaned down and planted a smacking kiss on her cheek. "Food was great, Momma. And thanks for the idea. Simon is kind of limited with his arm in a sling."

The woman who mothered everyone in the house stared at Simon for a long minute. "That boy needs a nap. He doesn't look like he slept on the boat."

Santiago looked at Lei Lu, and they both laughed.

"That child moves at a hundred miles an hour," Lei Lu claimed. "After the morning we've had, I think *I* need a nap."

"I'm going to go for a swim," Santiago announced and headed out the door toward the beach.

Lei Lu turned for the stairs, then looked over her shoulder at Tori and Nita. "Tag, you're it. You're on Simon duty."

Nita waited for the panic to start. She took inventory of her body, expecting the clinch of her esophagus right behind her heart. Nothing. There was no tightness in her stomach nor rising bile. Maybe it was because he was older and was capable of speech. If Simon were sick, he could tell her what hurt, what didn't feel good. She glanced up the stairway then down toward Daniel's room. Baby Bella couldn't tell her anything.

"*Mith* Nita, *Rothita thay* I need a nap. You read me a book and tuck me in?" He looked at her with those big blue eyes. Daniel's eyes set in such an innocent face. She couldn't say no. To the child or the father.

"Go grab a book, and I'll read it to you in your room." When Simon sprinted off toward the box that had suddenly appeared this morning, overflowing with age-appropriate toys, Nita stood and stretched once again. She hadn't slept well last night so a nap might be in her immediate future as well.

The child didn't find sleep until two books later. Nita stepped into the hall and left the door cracked open. Simon had been assigned one room down from Daniel's. Glancing two doors down to her own room, she turned to stare at the double doors to Daniel's suite.

She really should go in and check on baby Bella. Kira had left on the flight that morning with the others and might not be back for hours. Grace probably needed to take a break, too. Had somebody brought her lunch? She really should go check on the doses of medication that were being given to the baby.

Nita took one step, and her whole body revolted. Her stomach flipped. Shivering, sweat dripped down her temples. She couldn't seem to gasp in enough fresh air. She could hear every heartbeat pulse through her ears.

Her physician's brain kicked in to analyze her symptoms. Even though she'd taken every precaution, had she contracted Ebola? Taking two steps backward, she leaned against the wall.

Instantly, her body calmed. Within ten beats, her heart rate was back to normal. She no longer shook nor sweated. Gathering her wits, and her fortitude, she pushed off the wall and headed toward Daniel's suite and the baby.

She hadn't taken two steps and darkness closed in. The door that was only five feet away, seemed to be at the end of a long, darkening tube. She was panting so hard she almost passed out.

She was having a fucking panic attack.

One of the double doors opened and Grace quietly slid out. Shutting the door with barely a snick, she looked almost as surprised as Nita was when their eyes met. "Are you okay?" Her friend rushed to her. "You don't look so well."

"I'm not feeling very great either." Nita was not about to share the fact that she couldn't force her body to walk into that bedroom to care for that baby. Turning her back to the doors, and the situation, Nita made her way to her bedroom. "I think I'm just going to lie down for a while." Realization dawned on her. "Who's in with baby Bella?"

Grace smiled. "Tori came up to relieve me for lunch and brought up a fresh bottle. I never would've guessed she had such mothering instincts, but she snatched the baby up and plopped down in that rocker as if she'd done it a thousand times."

"Who'd-a thunk it?" Nita stepped into her room closing the door behind her, stripped out of every stitch of clothing, and crawled naked into her bed. The thousand-count sheets felt like silk on her nipples that instantly hardened. The thought of sliding into bed with Daniel beside her made her go wet at her core. She closed her eyes. Her last regret was that she was alone.

CHAPTER 11

"FROM THE PICTURES YOU SENT US, IT LOOKS AS THOUGH streets are paved with dead bodies." Tom's grim face filled the left half of the large flat screen above the dining room table. "Please tell me these weren't random shots, but were designated sites for disposal."

"I wish I could, sir, but we just snapped pictures as we walked through both Managua and San Miguelito." Daniel couldn't explain the assault on his other senses as they had talked to the sick and dying. The stench of vomit, shit, and decaying bodies weakened even his cast-iron stomach.

"Lieutenant Commander Callahan, did you see much looting, destruction of private property, or any roving gangs?" General Lyon, Commanding Officer of USSOCOM, asked from the right half of the screen. "Do I need to send in special operators?"

"No, sir, to all your questions," Katlin answered from across the table. Sometimes Daniel forgot that his sister was still on active duty serving in the Navy. "I think they're too sick to do much of anything. Now, that's not to say that when they start recovering and feeling better that we're not going to see illegal activity."

"Agent Callahan, I understand that you had a front row view of the EMP release. Give me your reactions." When the general leaned back in his chair the squeal was so loud Daniel barely withheld a wince.

There was silence for a long moment as he stared at his sister. He hadn't been aware she'd been close to the explosion.

"Daniel, you are Agent Callahan." His sister pointed a finger at him.

Fuck. No one had addressed him as agent since his original CIA training over fifteen years ago.

"Sorry, General Lyon, after being undercover for so many years I'm not used to anyone using that kind of formality." Daniel proceeded to give his impressions of the event. "Sir, I'm still not sure of the delivery system. I listened very carefully for helicopter blades, a rocket, or something to indicate incoming. There was nothing that I can identify."

General Lyon smiled. "Excellent. We used highflying drones. Most EMPs are delivered on a nuclear warhead which doesn't go over real big with most of our allies. Thanks to the military's extensive development of drones, we now have an entire fleet that can fly in at sixty-thousand-feet, drop-down almost vertically and hover over the intended target. Then boom. We get greater coverage by releasing above the ground. We don't care that the pulse takes out the delivery system. Drones are cheap compared to rockets and helicopters."

It was no wonder Daniel hadn't heard anything that night.

"I'm just glad we were far enough away not to be affected," Katlin interjected.

The general stared for five long seconds before he spoke.

"We waited until you were two deviations beyond the maximum range before sending the drones toward their targets. The Ladies of Black Swan, both teams, are far too-valuable assets to even take that chance."

"Thank you, sir." The relief on Katlin's face couldn't be ignored.

"If you'll excuse me, I need to report to POTUS." Tom didn't look excited about talking to the President of the United States about the recent findings. "The new Nicaraguan government is in crisis, and they are asking us for help. By the looks of the information you two have sent us, we need to act immediately."

"Don't send anyone down here unless they've had that magic shot," Daniel reminded them.

"Good point. I'll get some more CDC scientists on their way down to the Costa Rican lab." Tom typed for a moment. "They will need to use local subjects to start synthesizing the antiviral serum. General, we might need some of your teams to accompany the scientists into infected areas looking for recovered and healthy subjects."

"I think Marines are better suited for that job." The squeal of the chair was deafening as the general leaned forward. "Tom, you're going to have to make that suggestion to the president. I really can't be any part of it. I'd rather hold my men back for when they're truly needed."

"Agreed." Tom nodded. "I need to make that call, now. DD CIA out."

The uniformed man with stars on his shoulders filled the screen. "Lieutenant Commander Callahan, Agent Callahan, good work out there today. Katlin, all teams need rest tonight. I'm sending you both back out tomorrow. CO SOCOM out."

"Well, that—" Daniel started to say.

Katlin put her index finger over her lips and tilted her

head slightly toward Lei Lu who was typing so fast her hands seemed to blur.

Daniel glanced up at the screen where a Black Swan logo grew out of a distant point.

"And…we're clear." Lei Lu raised her hands into the air and stretched flexing her fingers several times. "Looks like we're not going anywhere for a couple of days. You want me to go over to the hotel and tell team two to hang tight?"

"Sure, I'd appreciate that." Katlin stood and peeled off the top to her black flight suit. "Part of me wants to burn these clothes, and the other part just wants a long hot shower."

"Uhm, Katlin, you do remember that flight suits don't burn. That's why we wear them." Lei Lu stood and closed her laptop before she started disconnecting wires.

"Sorry, sis, but I don't think any amount of soap and water and scrubbing, is going to get rid of the heebie-jeebies that were crawling under my skin all day, but good luck with that." But a shower was next on Daniel's agenda, too.

He'd felt so dirty that as soon as they'd pulled into the compound, he'd stripped down to the board shorts he'd worn under coveralls as he sprinted across the beach and dove into the warm Caribbean Sea. The salt water felt cleansing as he cleared his mind of the devastation he'd seen all day.

While Lei Lu had set up for the videoconference, he'd run upstairs to check on his kids and grab a T-shirt. Since Simon was still asleep and Bella was in Tori's competent hands, he was confident leaving them while he talked to the brass. He was damn glad the deep mahogany dining table hid his colorful shorts and bare legs. Caribbean casual could never be construed as professional dress.

With his duties over for the day, he had a little free time on his hands before supper.

Daniel and Katlin took different sides of the sweeping

staircase since their suites were on opposite ends of the building. As he walked down the hall, he remembered Grace mentioning that Nita wasn't feeling well. Deciding to check on her, he lightly knocked. When she didn't answer, he became more concerned. He'd slept for twenty-four straight hours when fighting off the effects of Ebola, even with the magical shot. She was going to need to be hydrated. If she were sick to her stomach, Kira could give her some medicine.

His rational seemed logical, but he just wanted to see her. Glancing down the hall, his sister had already disappeared into her room and no one else was around when he silently slid into her room on bare feet.

She lay on her side facing away from him, her beautiful brown curls contrasting against the yellow sheets and pillowcase. He wanted to check to see if she had a temperature, so he quietly stepped next to the bed.

She rolled over on a sigh and called out his name.

Good. She knows I'm here. He ran his fingers through her soft curls, raking them away from her face. "I'm right here, Angel."

He slowly rubbed his thumb over her cheek. She didn't feel either hot or cold and didn't seem to be sweating. Maybe she was just tired.

Then she moaned.

He leaned down to place a chaste kiss on her forehead, but at the last minute she lifted her face to meet his lips. She took the kiss deeper, and he let her. When she opened her mouth and their tongues danced and twisted. He ran his tongue over hers, and she explored his mouth until all he could taste was her. Holding her head in both hands, he tilted it the way he wanted for better access. Heated passion ignited like a match thrown on a gasoline-soaked bonfire. His desire for this woman exploded in a way he'd never experienced before.

Daniel had wanted women, and had women hundreds of times, but with Nita it was already different. Before, sex had always been...sex. Nothing more than a physical release. An opportunity to make his body, and the woman's, feel wonderful for a short time. An opportunity to forget the world around them, focusing completely on the momentary ecstasy they could bring to each other.

It had never meant anything emotional to him or his lover.

But Nita meant something to him. He couldn't define what that was, nor wanted to, as the taste of her flowed through his veins leaving tiny deposits in his heart. He needed more. He wanted to tangle their bodies the way their tongues thrust and retreated. His hands itched to explore every inch of her body the way he'd discovered every nook and crevice of her mouth.

Tearing his lips from hers he started a journey from the corner of her mouth kissing his way down her jaw to suck her earlobe.

"Oh, Daniel. More." Her whispered demand was permission for him to keep going.

But he wasn't sure he should.

Needing breath and wanting to at least slow things down, if not stop completely, he kissed her tenderly before he tore his mouth away from hers. As he gave them both some distance, he wondered what the hell he was doing. Well, he knew what he was doing and was damn good at it, but he questioned the sanity of seducing one of his sister's friends. Nita was also his friend, and he wanted to kiss his friend. In truth, he wanted to do a lot more than kiss her.

This wasn't a good idea. His son was asleep across the hall and his daughter was in the care of his sister's friends less than thirty feet away. Admittedly, they were all behind closed doors, and they were all adults, but…

"I…I should…" He dragged in a ragged breath and took a step back. "I should probably go."

"Stay." Nita's husky voice was like a caress of fingers along his shaft.

Daniel didn't move. "I just came in to check on you. Grace said you weren't feeling well."

"I was just a little tired." She shifted over, making room for him on the bed. "We've been putting in some really long hours getting the lab set up and finally running tests. I haven't really been sleeping well at night."

"Me either," he admitted before he thought better of it.

He glanced toward the unlocked the door and reassured himself that no one would enter Nita's room without knocking. Fuck. He hadn't cared about someone catching him mid-stroke since he was in college. They were all adults. Did he really give a shit if someone knew that he and Nita were attracted to each other?

No. He paused as he stared at the woman in the bed.

He didn't care about his reputation, but he cared about hers. What would her friends think of her, allowing their team leader's brother to fuck her? Of course they would treat her differently, perhaps even despise her. Hurting her was the last thing he wanted for Nita.

"Stay with me." The need in her voice was his affirmation but he still had to ask.

"Are you sure?" He left their next step up to her.

"I'm sure I want you in my bed." She raised an eyebrow. There was no doubt in those determined hazel eyes of hers.

Nita lifted the blankets, inviting him to crawl in. As he slid between the sheets, he reached for her. His hand found bare skin at her waist. He ran his hand up her back, then all the way down her spine, and over her perfectly rounded ass.

She was naked.

He couldn't believe it. He threw back the covers and slowly dragged his gaze the length of the most gorgeous body he'd ever seen. Her olive skin was different from his over-tanned, almost leather-colored body, at least the parts that had been exposed to the tropical sun far too often. His ass, on the other hand, was as white as the day he was born.

"Christ, Nita. You're beautiful." He cupped her breasts in both hands before bending his head and taking one of those dark nipples into his mouth. As he had with her tongue, he circled and toyed with it, then finally filled his mouth and sucked hard. When her back arched, forcing him to take more in his hand and mouth, he tucked away the fact that she enjoyed the way he taunted her breasts. He wondered what other erogenous zones she had waiting for him to discover.

He switched sides so as to give each breast equal treatment before he kissed his way over her flat stomach to her navel. He circled her innie with his tongue and thrust the tip hard against the indentation, then lightly pinched her nipples.

Her hips rose eight inches off the bed. Oh, yeah, she liked that.

Placing open-mouthed kisses all over her belly, he made his way to the neatly trimmed dark curly hair just above her sex. He could smell her arousal. His cock throbbed with the need to be sheathed inside her and feel her walls pulse with her release.

But she had to come first. He would always put her needs before his own.

With his thumbs, he spread her lips revealing her engorged clit to him. He kissed her most sensitive spot and she gasped. Then he licked from her opening to just below her clit and circled the bud.

She called his name just above a whisper. He wasn't sure if it was a plea, a warning, or a threat.

"Right here, angel." And he repeated the move. Then again and again.

"Please," she called.

He grinned and nipped her clit. "I'm still here." Looking up her quivering body, into her eyes, he taunted, "Do you want me to stop?"

"Fuck, no." She growled. "I want you inside me."

Obliging her, he slid two fingers into her slick, wet channel and sucked on her clit. Pumping them in and out, her body tightened around him, especially the muscles that gripped and released around his fingers.

He raised his head enough to see her hands fisted in the sheets at her sides. Her chest rose and fell as though she'd been sprinting. She was stunning. "I want to taste you as you come. Let yourself go, angel."

He watched her expression as he blew a stream of cool air over her heated sex. Her eyes widened in surprise just before he took her clit into his mouth and licked the underside. At the same time, he added another finger and shoved them inside her as far as he could.

She shuddered and shattered, drenching his mouth in her release. Moving quickly up her body, he took her mouth with a vicious kiss, silencing her scream. Rubbing her clit with his thumb and working his fingers in and out, he helped her ride out the orgasm until she grabbed his hand.

"Enough," she whispered between pants. "No more, please."

Using the pad of his thumb, he circled her clit. It

immediately hardened. "Oh, I think you could be encouraged to go again."

She curled into him and regained her breath. When she finally looked up at him, her smile was pure satisfaction. "You're damn good at that. I don't think I've ever come that hard before." She licked her lips. "I can taste myself." Her eyes turned devious. "Turnabout is fair play."

She stroked the length of his cock.

The door across the hall opened with a bang.

"*Mith* Nita. I'm awake. I'm done with my nap." Simon's voice cut through Daniel's sex-fogged brain.

The patter of his three-year-old little boy on the hall tile was his next warning.

"*Mith* Nita. Can we now go for a boat ride?"

Daniel leaped out of the bed a second before his son burst though the bedroom door. Blue eyes met his. "Hi, Daddy. You want to come on a boat ride with me and *Mith* Nita? She can drive a boat."

His son didn't think it was strange that his father was standing in Nita's bedroom.

He dared a glance at the woman he could still taste and realized that she'd pulled the covers up to her chin and kept her head on the pillow.

"I think Nita is tired from all her recent activity." He put his hand on his son's shoulder. "Let's let her sleep a little longer while we see if Rosita has a snack for us."

"I like *nack*, 'pecially the kind from *Mith Rothita*." He looked up at Daniel. "And you 'posed to call them *Mith* Nita and *Mith Rothita*. Aunt Katlin told me that."

Daniel laughed as he turned his son toward the door. Their mother had taught Daniel and Katlin to add Miss and Mister to the first name of adults as a show of respect. Leave it to his sister to teach his kid manners. Simon's own mother sure as hell didn't.

"Son, why don't you go down stairs and find Ro— Miss Rosita. I'll be right there. I want to check on your sister first."

"Okay, Daddy." The boy took off.

Daniel strode to the bed. "I'm sorry." He ran the back of his knuckles down the side of her cheek.

Astonishment fell over her face like a dark veil. "I'm not. I don't regret anything we did."

Fuck. She misunderstood. He ran his fingers into her soft hair and bent over, his lips an inch from hers. "I'm sorry my son interrupted us." He grinned. "I haven't even got started on everything I want to do to you, for you, and with you."

He closed his eyes to everything in the outside world and laid his lips on hers. Forcing himself to make it brief, he stood and turned before he opened his eyes. He couldn't look back as he left the room. If he did, he'd want to run back and crawl in that bed with her and finish everything they started and never leave until he'd run down his grocery list of ways he wanted to make love to her.

And he loved her…as a friend…with benefits.

He turned toward his suite to check on his precious baby Bella.

CHAPTER 12

Nita sat at the dining room table, the large flat screen filled with boxes. In the upper left, a virologist from the CDC was ordering equipment to be sent to the clean room in Costa Rica. In the center at the top was the Chief of Internal Medicine at Walter Reed National Military Medical Center. He and Nita were currently working out estimated numbers of viable patients, best practices for treatment, and medications needed.

She glanced at the poor guy on the lower left who kept growing the list on the lower right. Tom Callahan had tasked him with the duty to find, buy, rent, or obtain by other means, everything she needed. Then, the Director of Logistics for the CIA had to get it to her immediately.

"Dr. Banks, I'd like to send down more researchers. Can your clean room handle more people?" the CDC doctor asked.

"It's small," Nita admitted, almost ready to turn down his offer. Then she remembered just how tired the team she'd rescued out of Nicaragua was becoming. Working against the clock, each researcher had pushed themselves to their physical limits. "But I think if we worked around the clock, changing shifts every six hours so everyone could eat and rest, we'd be able to expand the number of tests which should logically result in finding a cure faster. Please send fifteen more people."

"You have accommodations for that many more or do I need to send tents?"

Nita had to withhold her laugh. With the resort's location so close to the Nicaraguan border and the coup that had made worldwide news within hours, dozens of tourists had canceled their reservations at the resort next door. Fortunately, they'd been able to keep a lid on the Ebola epidemic.

When General Cortez closed the Nicaraguan borders, he told the international press that it was so his new government could assure tourists' safety. It wasn't a lie…exactly. There had been rumors about the former presidential guard reorganizing and mounting an attempt to free the president from his imprisonment.

The EMP had effectively silenced any communication from the old capital of Managua. The general had casually mentioned that many people were suffering from a midsummer influenza. It happened every year about this time according to his press secretary. Spin doctoring at its best.

If the world had any idea of the size of the Ebola epidemic Nicaragua was facing, tourism from the Mexican Yucatán Peninsula, north to Southern California, and south to the Panama Canal, would cease to exist. Most of those countries depended on the billions of dollars generated by foreigners adorning their ancient cities and spending their modern money. The entire Central American monetary system could collapse.

Nita got everyone on the screen to agree to the priority

ranking of the list before she sent them back to work and shut down the videoconference.

How the hell had she become in charge of containing an epidemic? With the weight of the daunting job ahead, Nita folded her arms on the table and rested her head. Too many thoughts. Too much responsibility. Too much depended on every one of her decisions.

She needed a drink. Just one. She had to keep her thoughts clear.

"*Mith* Nita." A small hand lightly patted her shoulder as the sweet voice cut through her heavy thoughts. "*Mith* Nita, *Mith Rothita* told me to bring this to you."

She rolled her head to the side to look into the innocent face. She saw that he was holding a tall glass filled with ice and a thick orangeish-pink liquid. Sitting up, she took the glass from Simon, recognizing it as one of the fruity cocktails Katlin had created during the month they'd been sequestered in the compound while waiting for USSOCOM teams to eliminate a terrorist who had put a contract out on the Ladies of Black Swan. Nita couldn't remember what Katlin had named it, but one sip assured that the rum-laden punch truly packed a punch.

"You *thick*, *Mith* Nita?" Simon asked openly. "I put my head down when I don't feel good too."

Nita smiled and realized how wonderful she felt all the way to her soul. "Well, Simon, I am thick," she readily admitted. She'd never been thin or skinny. "I like to think of myself as solid and compact." Then added, "But I'm not sick." She emphasized the *s*.

"Good." Simon crawled right up in her lap as though the fact she wasn't sick gave him permission to do so. He threw his good arm around her neck and turned to look into her eyes.

Oh, Christ. Those eyes, so much like his father's, threw her momentarily. She'd forgotten, just for a second, this adorable little boy was Daniel's son. She wasn't sure how long it would take her to get used to the fact that he had children and never told anyone, not even his sister.

His lie of omission hurt. She considered Daniel a friend, a good friend, yet he hadn't trusted her enough to tell her about his children. She wondered, not for the first time, if their mother hadn't died would he have left them to their life in Nicaragua? Would he ever have discovered how abusive their mother had been?

Nita didn't exactly believe in predetermined destiny, but she was sure that God would never have left those children without Daniel in their life. She also believed, deep in her soul, that these children had been brought to her for a reason. Since discovering the abuse Simon had endured, his reason for being there had been revealed.

She glanced up the stairs as though she could see into Daniel's suite. Was it her destiny to help baby Bella?

With a ding, an e-mail from the CIA logistician popped up on her computer. When she reached for the keys, Simon started to get down. "It's okay," she reassured him. "Stay right there. This will only take a minute. Yes," she said with a satisfied smile. The top priority items had been secured and would be on a plane headed to them tonight along with several of the next level items. She dashed off a quick thank you and closed her computer.

After a sip of her much-needed drink, Nita focused on the child in her lap. "We have an hour before supper. Want to go for a swim?"

Simon's entire face lit up with excitement. Then his shoulders dropped on a huff as he stared down at his sling in disappointment. "Can't."

"Sure you can. Hop down," she ordered. Taking his good hand, they headed toward the kitchen. "I'm pretty sure Rosita has dealt with broken bones before. I'll bet she has a plastic bag of some kind we can wrap around your cast that will help keep it waterproof.

Ten minutes later, they were both headed upstairs to their rooms to change into bathing suits.

"Can Daddy come, too?" Simon practically begged.

Nita didn't care one way or the other. "He's pretty busy right now, you can go ask. Knock quietly so you don't wake baby Bella if she's sleeping."

Without letting go of her hand, Simon dragged her to the door of Daniel's suite. "You knock. He won't get mad at you."

Concerned, Nita kneeled to look the boy face-to-face. "Has your daddy ever gotten mad at you and hurt you?"

Simon shook his head fervently. "No. Mama *thay* we can't interrupt Daddy. He important." His face squinted as though seriously thinking. "We're not back in camp anymore. We're here in our new home. Is Daddy important here?"

Nita burst out laughing. "Your daddy is still important, but I'm sure we can interrupt him to see if he wants to go swimming with us." Nita wondered how much actual time Daniel spent with his son.

Simon threw both arms around Nita and held her tight. "Thank you, *Mith* Nita."

She stood up with the boy in her arms, and he wrapped his thin legs around her waist. Boldly she stepped up to the door and tapped. "Daniel, may we come in?"

"Sure," he called in a normal voice. "I'm just giving Bella a bottle."

When she stepped into the room, her heart clenched at the sight of the big man in the rocking chair holding the tiny child so tenderly. Simon climbed out of her arms and walked carefully toward them. His eyes were not on his father, but his sister. Nita's heart broke just a little as Simon's gaze traveled up the tube to the bag hanging over the nearby crib.

His jaw quivered in the way only small children can do. "Bella not better?"

Before Daniel answered, his eyes met Nita's. She had no idea whether the baby was improving or not. She hadn't even been in to check the child. Except for the few brief moments when Daniel had first handed her Bella, she'd never even looked at his baby.

She looked away and saw a clipboard at the end of the crib. Hoping it was some kind of a chart, she walked over and studied the top sheet.

Fuck.

No. Bella wasn't getting better. Nita studied the chart of temperature, respiration, heartbeat, and food intake.

"Knock, knock," Kira's cheery voice came from the open door. She looked from Daniel, Simon, and the baby to Nita. "I'm glad you're here." She stepped beside Nita and pointed to the temperature column. "The baby Tylenol doesn't seem to be keeping the fever down for very long. Twice, I've had to give her cool baths while waiting for the next round to take effect. She's not eating much either, and I've tried every trick I learned during my neonatal ICU rotation."

Nita flipped through a few pages. "I don't see any labs."

Shock was written across Kira's pretty face. "Is there a hospital lab close by that we can use? Dan—I was told the nearest hospital was an hour and a half away by airplane."

"The nearest hospital is that far, but we have a state-of-the-art lab two-hundred feet down the beach." Nita glanced at the baby in Daniel's arms then quickly returned her gaze back to Kira. "I was never any good at finding those tiny veins.

Would you take a blood sample from her, please? I'll be more than happy to take it over to the lab and get them working on it right away."

"Yes, ma'am." Kira went to a box of infant medical supplies that had been shipped down.

"In this house, we don't stand on military protocol," Daniel informed both women. "The only person who has rank here is Rosita, and she is the queen of everything."

"That *Mith Rothita*. Aunt Katlin *thaid tho*." Simon glared at his father as though he should've known.

"My point is made." Daniel readjusted Bella into one hand and pulled his son onto his other knee. "Out of the mouths of babes." He then focused his complete attention on Simon. "Did you come in here to see your sister and me?"

"No, *Mith* Nita and me going *thimming*." He proudly showed his father the plastic-wrapped arm. "Can you go with *uth*?"

"How about I take Miss Bella while you go spend some time with your son?" Kira kneeled down so she could be on Simon's level. "That water is wonderful. It's warm and clear and just about perfect."

"You already been *thimming, Mith* Kira?" Simon was such a friendly child and so curious.

"Yes, we swam as a team this morning. Three miles." Kira cocked her head. "Do you know how to swim?"

Simon gave her a huge smile and proudly declared, "I *thim* in the bathtub."

"Looks like I need to add swimming to the list of things I have to teach you," Daniel said as he handed Kira the baby. He held up a nearly full bottle. "She didn't drink much, and she needs to burp."

Kira immediately flopped a hand towel on to her shoulder

and positioned Bella. A few gentle back rubs and a couple of pats was all it took.

He lifted Simon off his knee. "Teaching you to pronounce *s* is my first priority." He looked at his son for a long moment then grimaced. "We didn't bring many clothes with us, did we?"

Simon slowly shook his head. "No, Daddy. But *Mith Rothita* give me a lot of *thirt* and *thort*. They are in my drawer. Want to *thee*?" He took Daniel by the hand and dragged him toward the door.

"Give me a few minutes to change and run Bella's blood sample over to the lab." Nita gave what she hoped was an encouraging smile. "I'll meet you at the beach."

"See you there." Daniel disappeared through the door.

Simon's excitement could be heard all the way down the hall to his room.

Kira held out Bella. "If you'll hold her, I'll see if I can get a vein in this other arm."

Nita's stomach flipped over as bile rose up her throat. Damn it. She was going to puke. Sweat beaded on her brow as her lungs closed down. She couldn't take that baby. Her hands were shaking so bad she shoved them in her pockets. There was no way in hell she could hold that baby. Thinking quickly she suggested, "Let's put her in the crib, and I'll hold her down."

Kira shrugged and laid the baby in the crib.

Nita truly hated this. She hated herself for not being physically able to hold the baby. She hated Daniel for bringing the child to her. She hated God for making this poor baby sick.

Carefully, she held the child immobile while Kira expertly found a vein and filled the tube. "She's so dehydrated, I really don't want to take any more than this. Do you think it will be enough?"

"Absolutely." Nita shook the tube visually examined color and consistency. "It'll have to be."

Kira picked up Bella and cooed.

Nita was envious of the nurse practitioner. She couldn't do that. Not now. "You're very good with her."

"I like babies, but I hate to see them sick." Kira nestled the child into the feeding position and offered her the bottle once again. "I hope you find out what's wrong with her."

With a nod, Nita headed for the door. "The faster I get this into the lab, the faster we find out what's going on inside that beautiful little baby."

Nita slipped into her bathing suit and cover-up in minutes. On her way to the lab, she truly lucked out. Dr. James Johnson, the lead researcher, was on his way in, saving Nita from the clean room entering procedures. She gave him a list of tests she wanted him to run, and he suggested a few others that had shown promise in their experimentation. Nita would do anything to make that baby better.

She jogged the two hundred feet down the beach to where Simon sat in waist-deep water and splashed. His laughter carried on the wind. The tides didn't change much in the tropics, they simply creeped a few more feet up the white sand with slow gentle lapping.

In one practiced motion, she whipped off her cover-up and flung it on the chaise lounge close to the water's edge. Trotting over to Daniel and Simon, she sat in the sand on the other side of the boy who seemed to be building a sand castle that got washed away with every wave.

"This doesn't look much like swimming lessons," she accused Daniel.

His smile never faltered, and his gaze never left his son.

"It isn't. He was just having so much fun, I hated to ruin it." He leaned back on his elbows. "One of my first memories is of Mom and Dad taking me to the beach. I have a no idea where we were." He glanced over at Simon then back out at the ocean. "I think I was about Simon's age. It was just the three of us then. We were there to cheer Mom up." He was quiet for a long minute. "She'd probably just lost another baby. I know there were several between me and Katlin."

Daniel was silent, so Nita decided to occupy Simon's attention. They built a bigger castle, digging in the warm sand with their hands, then giggling as the next wave knocked it over and flattened it out.

Simon glanced over at his father and leaned back on his good elbow, gently laying the casted arm across his stomach. In that moment they looked so much alike, yet so different. Daniel had hard firm muscles, everywhere. In that position, his six-pack abs looked like rolling hills under skin tanned to a rich gold. His dark wavy hair a few inches too long, covered most of his ears. His angular face and strong jaw hadn't seen a razor in years, but he kept the mustache and beard neatly trimmed.

Memories of those soft curly hairs tickling her thighs made her wet, and it wasn't from the ocean water that moved up and down her legs.

Daniel looked over at her and scratched his beard as though he'd known what she'd been thinking.

Mimicking his father, Simon scratched his baby soft cheeks.

Daniel scratched his belly, and Simon mirrored the movement.

Nita couldn't help herself. She threw her head back and laughed. This damn kid was so much fun. She looked at her watch and saw that they only had about twenty minutes before supper time. "You ready to learn to swim now?"

Simon looked at the water. "The ocean a lot bigger than the bathtub."

Damn, he cracked her up, but she tried to hold a straight face. "Yep. It certainly is, and that's what makes it so wonderful. Once you learn to swim on top of the water, and you grow a little bit bigger, I'll teach you to swim under the water like a fish."

"I can hold my breath and blow bubble. Want to *thee*?" Simon rolled over onto his belly and made a production of taking a very deep breath and putting his lips under the water. About that time the wave withdrew, and he was blowing air.

"I don't see any bubbles." Nita pointed out toward deeper water. "Let's go out there and you can show me real bubbles."

Daniel rolled over, scooped up his son on the way to his feet, and started to wade out into the clear Caribbean water. Nita rose quickly and walked beside them, stopping when they were knee-deep.

"You can stand up here," Daniel reassured his son as he gently set him down in the water.

Wide-eyed, Simon swallowed hard but said nothing. He was being extremely brave. Nita wasn't sure if it was to impress her or his father. Daniel never let go, holding him securely just under his arms.

"Okay, Simon. Let's see those bubbles," she challenged.

The boy looked a little bit apprehensive, so she kneeled down next to him. She sucked in a dramatic breath, stuck her whole face in the water, and started blowing bubbles. When she came up for air, she sluiced away the water with her hand. "Your turn."

She saw the hesitation in his face. "Maybe your daddy

needs to show you how to do it." Nita gave Daniel raised eyebrows and an unspoken dare.

"Hold on to him." Daniel stepped from behind Simon and kneeled next to him. "She's just a girl. She doesn't know how to do this right. I'm going to teach you the way my dad taught me. Men and boys do it with noise." Daniel took a deep breath but when he put his lips under the water, he made engine noises with them. It actually sounded similar to a sports car right down to shifting gears.

"Okay, son, let's do this together." When Daniel started to inhale, Simon joined him. They lowered their chins at the same time until the watered just covered their lips. Daniel winked, and they both started making noises.

Well, damn, they were in harmony. In a tradition passed down from grandfather to father to son, it was a fucking hallmark moment.

Nita fell a little bit in love, with both Callahans.

CHAPTER 13

Nita had forgotten her cover-up on the chaise, so when she entered the house Daniel and Simon were nowhere to be seen.

As she headed for the steps, Rosita scooted out of the kitchen. "Nita, could you please take this up to baby Bella? I'm needed in the kitchen right now, and these old knees have a hard time with those steps."

"Certainly, I'm headed that way." Nita looked at the clear bottle. "What's in this, anyway?"

Rosita laughed. "It's an old recipe that's been in my family for probably a hundred years. You're a modern doctor, so you might not understand the old ways, but we've been settling upset tummies long before the Spanish conquerors ever came to this area."

"I'll admit, shots and pills aren't always the cure." She pinned Rosita with a hard stare. "How do you make this? I'm truly curious."

"Mostly fruits. The mountain man brings me elderberries, which can sometimes be a little tart, so I add orange juice and some cane sugar." She looked a little nervous, but added,

"Then there are a few spices that I add in as it cooks. I strain it so there are no seeds. I let it cool, but babies like things warm." She quickly added, "It's all good for her."

Nita smiled. "It sounds like it. The berries and oranges will give her plenty of vitamins C and D and the sugar will give her a boost of energy to help fight this off. I'm not sure which spices you're using, but I'm sure they're good for her. Probably makes it taste better, too. Let me get this up to her."

After knocking quietly, Nita cracked the door. Kira was taking Bella's temperature and recording all her vitals.

"Come on in," Kira called. "She's asleep, but I expect her to wake any minute. Thanks for bringing up the bottle."

Nita's gaze swept over the living room portion of Daniel's suite then glanced down the short hallway toward his bedroom before she heard the shower running. The thought of him naked, lathering soap and rubbing it all over his body made her wet. She could easily imagine her hands running over his chest, curving those powerful shoulders, then down over his hard abs, following that happy trail of dark hair to his—

"I take it you haven't heard back from the lab yet?" Kira's question shattered Nita's daydream.

"No, not yet. Some of the tests take twenty-four hours to run." Nita looked at the dark pink cheeks on the baby in the crib. "Is her fever back up?"

"I'm afraid so. The acetaminophen doesn't seem to last long for her, and I'm very careful not to overdose." She looked at Nita, nurse to doctor. "Given her weight, and that she's small for her age, I've calculated the dosage, but it doesn't even last four hours. I checked with a pediatrician friend of mine back at Walter Reed, and he cautioned me not to exceed the recommended daily amount."

"If we have to, we'll get the chief of neonatology on a

conference call, but he's going to want to know the results of those tests." She considered for a moment. "If we don't hear something in a couple hours, I'll go over to the lab myself."

Relief showed on Kira's face. "Thank you, Nita. When we got orders to come to Costa Rica to help out the Ladies of Black Swan team one, I never expected to be using these nursing skills. I thought I'd be patching people up, maybe working triage, perhaps even at the side of a surgeon in the operating room."

Nita chuckled. "I haven't been in a research lab in six years. I feel so awkward in there. But I'll do what I have to do to accomplish the mission." She patted Kira's well-muscled bicep. "Trust me, you'll see your share of blood and guts and gore. You'll also be the cause of plenty of it. Our jobs are far from pretty."

Returning to her own room, she stripped out of her bathing suit and tossed it over the towel rod. Stepping into the glassed-in shower with multiple heads, she scrubbed the salt water and sand off her body. Wrapped in a towel she headed toward her dresser.

At the light tap on her door she automatically called, "Come on in." She figured it was one of the women on her team. They had all seen each other naked more times than she could count. Without looking to see who'd entered, she dropped her towel and started digging through clothes in her dresser on the far side of the bed. When no one spoke. She glanced over to find Daniel standing motionless, staring at her.

He'd also seen her naked. She'd never been self-conscious about nudity, so she simply asked, "Is there something I can do for you?"

"Fuck, yes." He closed the distance to her and pulled her down onto the bed. "We never got to finish what we started."

She giggled like a virgin at this playful side of Daniel. "I believe you're wearing far too many clothes for this party."

His mouth crashed on hers, only leaving her lips to slide off his T-shirt. Naked chest to naked chest, he writhed above her as he shucked his shorts and tossed them next to her towel.

"I want to be inside you so bad my cock hurts." He attacked her breasts with his hands and mouth, rolling her nipples before lightly pinching them. Her hips automatically shot off the bed and found what they sought.

He was hard and ready. So was she. Daniel seemed to bring her from zero to ready in seconds. She didn't know how he had that effect on her, but at this point she really didn't care. She loved what he was doing to her.

He dragged his hand between her breasts over her stomach and cupped her mound. Dipping one finger down her wet slit he kissed her desperately before he lifted his head to stare into her eyes. "Do you want me anywhere near as much as I want you?"

She placed her hand over his and moved it down as she widened her legs. "What do you think?"

"I think you'd better have condoms somewhere close, or I'm going to have to make a trip to my bedroom and embarrass myself in front of whoever is watching Bella at the moment." He shoved two fingers inside her and moaned as he rocked his erection into her hip.

She reached for the nightstand, but her fingers couldn't quite make it to the knob on the drawer, so she flipped him over onto his back and retrieved a packet. Ripping it open with her teeth, she decided to tease him and slowly rolled it down his shaft, pumping a few times. Before he could move she straddled his hips and watched his face carefully.

He reached up and cupped a breast in each warm hand. "I

like this position." He gently massaged and rolled the nipples between his thumbs and forefingers. The way he touched her sent tingles straight to her clit. Then he pinched her nipples. Hard.

Her eyes flew open and she stared into his deep sapphire gaze. "Don't just sit there, angel. Ride me."

She normally didn't like taking orders in bed, unless it was one of the parameters determined ahead of time, but she wanted him inside her, now. She lifted up, and up some more, so she could take him in. At the last minute, she decided to tease him. Grabbing his shaft, she rubbed the tip of his cock from her opening to her clit and back again.

His shuddered intake of breath was her reward. So, she did it again. "I believe you like that."

"I like everything you do to me." Then he pulled her down and pressed her chest into his. "Way too much." He kissed her temple in the sweetest gesture any man had ever made. It was as though he truly cared for her, about her.

Then he ruined it.

He smacked her ass.

"Fucking ride me, or I'm going to flip you over onto your hands and knees and take you from behind."

She pushed up off his shoulders and gave him a slow grin. "And what makes you think I wouldn't absolutely love that?"

"I think you like to be in control of every situation." He held her gaze for a long minute. "I'm going to let you be in control of this one...this time." He sat up and wrapped his arms around her, pulling her in so her ear was next to his lips. "But if you don't slide onto my dick in the next minute, I'm going to have to get out of this bed and take care of the situation myself. In case you've forgotten, this house is filled with people who don't understand the meaning of a shut door."

He ran his tongue around the edge of her ear then sucked the lobe into his mouth. "Now," he kissed her jaw just below her ear. "Be the angel of mercy." Two more kisses on her jaw. "And let's finish this." He captured her mouth as his hands dropped to her hips.

She rose up and guided him to her entrance. In one swift movement he was completely inside her.

His fingers gripped her hips, hard. "Hold it. Right there." He squinted his eyes closed, and his face became a mask of torture. "I…didn't expect—" He gently squeezed and released his tight grip on her hips.

She contracted her Kegel muscles just to torture him. "Hold it like this?" she asked innocently.

He opened his eyes. "I'm serious, Nita. I need a minute if you want this to last." He glanced away. "It's been a while for me." He swallowed hard. "And you just feel so good. It's hot and soft inside you."

She relaxed her inner muscles. He was practically begging. She wondered how long it had really been?

When the tension in his face eased, she knew he had his body under control.

He slowly opened his eyes. "I want this to be good for you." He grinned. "I know it's gonna be great for me."

Well, damn. There he went again, being nice. Sex was supposed to be sex. She preferred it fast and dirty, done and gone. But nothing had been the same with Daniel.

"Okay. Time to move, angel." He reached down between them and circled her clit with his thumb.

She drew in a shaky breath and rose up, tightening every muscle from her butt cheeks through her thighs. She came back down and swore she felt him at the entrance to her womb. He pressed on her clit, and every muscle in her body tightened. It was the first time they'd done this, but it was as if she and Daniel had been having sex for years. He knew exactly what she liked and gave it to her when she needed it most.

She made every stroke count, keeping a tight grip around his cock. For some unbeknownst reason, she wanted to be the best he'd ever had. She wanted Daniel Callahan to remember these few minutes in her bed. Because they would probably be their last together. Neither was into long-term relationships.

"Are you close?" Daniel asked between pants.

"Almost there." She was so damn close, maybe two more strokes.

Daniel rubbed the length of her clit with the pad of his thumb, and her world blew apart. His large hand grasped the back of her head and pulled her lips to his. He kept rubbing and pressing hard as her entire body shook with what had to be the biggest orgasm she'd ever had in her life. It was definitely one of the longest. She was falling forward onto his shoulder when he arched up inside her one last time, stiffened and groaned through clenched teeth.

Nita lay sprawled on top of Daniel. His softening cock was still inside her when she recognized voices at the bottom of the stairs.

"Let me see if I can find Nita." Katlin's voice seemed to be coming closer. "I'll grab Daniel, too. I'm sure he's going to want to know what you found out."

Nita leaped out of bed. "Go into the bathroom," she ordered on a whisper.

He'd barely shut the door behind him when Katlin lightly tapped. "Hey Nita, Dr. Johnson has discovered something and is waiting for you downstairs. I think Daniel's going to want to hear this, too."

Naked, but unconcerned because both people in her room

had seen her naked on more than one occasion, Nita finished pulling clothes from her drawer. "Would you go entertain Dr. Johnson while I get dressed? I'll grab Daniel, and we'll be down in a few minutes."

Casually, Nita picked up her beach towel, slyly wrapping Daniel's board shorts and T-shirt so they were hidden inside.

"I can grab Daniel." Katlin turned to head out the room.

"Let me," Nita insisted. "I want to explain to him the tests that I had the lab run before we hear the results."

As though that made perfect sense, Katlin agreed and left the room heading back down to distract the researcher.

In her bathroom, she tossed the board shorts to Daniel who had already disposed of the condom. He turned on the water and cleaned up.

"That was close." Nita hung up her towel.

Daniel wrapped his arms around her from behind. "Would it bother you if Katlin found out?"

Nita turned in his arms and laid her palms on his chest. "You don't think it's weird to fuck one of your sister's good friends?"

"No." He placed his forehead on hers, which felt more intimate than the fact their bodies were naked and perfectly aligned. "I fucked one of *my* friends…and we both enjoyed it. I actually like this friends-with-benefits relationship. With you, once was not enough."

His cock twitched against her belly, and her clit ached for his touch.

He lightly brushed his lips across hers before releasing her. "But I can't have you the way I want right now. I need to know what that researcher found and if he can help Bella." He stepped away and slid on his shorts.

She wanted him again, but valued her relationship with his sister even more. She had no idea how Katlin would feel if she knew what Nita and Daniel had just done. The brother and sister were close. But, damn it, Nita didn't know if she could walk away from him. If she had to make a choice between the Ladies of Black Swan and Daniel, in that moment, she had no idea which choice she'd make.

Nita walked to her bed and laid out pretty pink boy short panties and a matching satiny-soft bra.

Daniel was instantly beside her. "Let me." He kneeled. "I've never dressed a woman before." Lifting her foot, he bent and kissed her ankle. "I've never wanted to either."

Kissing his way up her legs, he pulled up the panties, dragging his fingertips lightly the length of her legs, igniting every nerve ending. Wanting him again chased the need to meet their company throughout her entire body. When he nuzzled into the curls at the apex of her thighs, she nearly came. Using his thumbs, he parted her and placed a light kiss on her clit. She dropped her hands to the back of his head holding him there, begging for more.

He grinned up at her. "We have company waiting for us."

He kissed his way up to her breasts. After a nipping kiss on each nipple, he picked up the bra.

She slid her arms through the straps and he moved around to the back. "Which hook?"

"Second, please." She could barely speak. Lots of men had taken her clothes off her body, but Daniel was the first to put them on. It seemed even more sensual than stripping her.

Reaching around her, he slid his hands under her breasts, readjusting them in the cups. When he withdrew, her breasts felt chilled, missing the heat of his hands.

"Arms up," he commanded.

She did as asked, but before he dropped the T-shirt over her hands and head, he placed an open mouth kiss just above her belly button.

He grabbed the pink plaid shorts and kneeled in front of her. Although she could easily balance on her own, she laid her hands on his shoulders just so she could touch him one more time as she stepped into the shorts. His fingers dragged up her legs from ankles to thighs as he pulled the shorts up to her waist.

"We really have to go." Nita headed barefoot toward the door, but Daniel spun her around before she reached for the handle.

He gave her the most tender kiss she'd ever had. Grabbing her hand, he gave it one last squeeze before they walked into the hall.

"Now, Nita, what do I need to know about these tests?" Daniel dropped her hand.

She completely understood he'd done it for her.

CHAPTER 14

As they made their way down the wide staircase, Daniel watched Dr. James Johnson as he anxiously shifted his ample girth side-to-side. The iced tea nearly sloshed over the rim of the tall glass he held in his left hand. A stack of papers filled his right.

"Good afternoon, James. I hope your presence here means good news for all of us." Nita seemed friendly toward the fiftyish man. "I don't believe you've formally met Daniel Callahan. He looks a bit different without the camouflage grease paint, but he helped us escape from Managua. The samples I sent over were from his six-month-old daughter."

"Thank you, Mr. Callahan." James look surprised to find both hands full. He started to move the papers into the crook of his arm when Nita plucked them from his hand. Daniel took the now empty hand in a firm shake.

"I thought we were goners there for a minute. Okay, more like ten minutes, but it felt like hours when they were shooting at us." James shook his head. "I never want to be involved in anything like that again."

"None of us do." Daniel gestured toward the dining room

table fearing he was going to end up wearing that iced tea if James didn't set it down soon. "Have a seat."

With a grateful sigh, the researcher moved in that direction. Without even thinking, Daniel moved to the head of the table, his usual spot, and gestured for the man to sit on his left. When Nita started to pull out a chair on the far side of the doctor, he motioned toward the chair on his right. It wasn't that he was jealous of her working relationship with James, he simply wanted her close to him. "Come sit by me."

Realizing it sounded too much like an order, Daniel added the word, "Please."

She stood next to the chair for one heartbeat, then two. He gave her a small smile and saw the hardness in her hazel eyes melt. She scanned the entire main floor as she circled the table. He felt her light touch across his shoulders before she rounded the edge and sat next to him.

Daniel normally didn't like public displays of affection, but Nita's touch soothed him. He didn't realize he'd been so anxious, but he'd been around Bella more in the past forty-eight hours then he'd ever been. His life in camp had been focused on Cristobal and his men. He'd taken time to go see his kids, and on occasion their mother would dump them on him, but he'd never been solely responsible for them for more than a few hours.

His little baby girl was very sick, and he could do nothing to help her.

Christ, he sucked as a father.

James shuffled papers and finally extracted one from the pile. "Your daughter is already on a regiment of antivirals which normally shorten the illness's affect, as well as antibiotics which help prevent serious complications such as pneumonia." He slid the paper toward Daniel and pointed to a list of words, each at least eight syllables in length, next to numbers.

"This is one of the most potent antivirals available," Nita explained. She pointed to the number next to it. "I've kept its dosage relatively low because of Bella's weight." Under the table she laid her hand over his. "It's never been tested in infants before, but it's been proven effective in children over the age of five. Basically, it keeps the virus from attaching itself to other new healthy cells."

Daniel rolled his hand over and interlaced his fingers with hers and gave it a squeeze. "I'm sure you're doing everything you can to make her better."

Nita lowered her eyelids for just a moment before returning her gaze to his. She pointed to the next item on the list. "This is just a big word for baby Tylenol. It helps keep her fever down which allows her body to fight off the infection. It also makes her feel a little better, too. I've talked with Kira at length about how much were giving her, because we have to be careful not to overdose her."

He squeezed her hand in understanding. "Thank you."

"This next one is a steroid which gives her body a little boost and—"

"Aren't steroids bad for you?" Daniel looked from Nita to James.

"Technically, they can be." James took off his glasses and started to clean them with the edge of his shirt.

"She won't suddenly develop Hulk-like muscles or go into a roid rage when something pisses her off," Nita reassured him. "These are a totally different kind of steroid. Moving on." She went through every item on the list, explaining each medication. Daniel was no dummy. He'd been a member of Mensa since he was in high school, but he didn't need to know the chemistry and physiology behind the medicine they were giving his daughter.

When Nita had completed the list, she slid it back across the table.

James extracted another sheet. "For most Americans, my next suggestion is going to sound archaic, but I've worked endemics, epidemics, and pandemics all over the world and sometimes local remedies are the most effective. When we were up in the northern regions of Nicaragua, where the Ebola outbreak first happened, we had a young biologist with us who noticed the monkeys suddenly eating more cat's claw."

He lifted his eyes and looked directly into Daniel's. "The Reston Ebola virus started in monkeys. We didn't think it could spread to humans, but it did, and was even more deadly. The indigenous people of that area didn't get help soon enough, nor did they accept our help when we arrived… so many died." James slowly shook his head.

Panic ripped through Daniel. For the first time, he realized he could lose his baby girl. A vice clamped around his heart. He could hardly breathe. He wanted to run upstairs, scoop Bella out of her crib, and hold her, using his own sheer will to force her to get better.

Nita reached up and turned his chin, so he faced her. "You brought Bella to me, and we got her the best medical care on this planet. You can't get any more leading-edge research than the clean room that's two hundred feet down that beach." She glanced over at James then back at Daniel. "I think we should listen to what James is about to propose."

Daniel felt considerably better. Her touch alone calmed him. He turned his attention toward James.

"Okay, I was telling you about cat's claw. It's a vine that one of the other researchers up north saw the monkeys eating like crazy." He shuffled through the pile while continuing to talk. "The other team collected and analyzed the chemistry of both leaves and flowers, but the flowers weren't any good, but the leaves contained high amounts of—"

"I don't give a fuck what it contained." Daniel's impatience had reached its limit. "Cut to the bottom line. What does all of this have to do with saving my daughter?"

Daniel's angry tone didn't seem to bother Dr. Johnson. He replaced the piece of paper in the pile and dug out another. "Chyna thinks that we should supplement modern medicine with some ancient techniques."

"We're talking Chyna, the intern, right?" Nita sounded hesitant.

"Yes." James nodded. "She's quite a brilliant biologist. Her master's thesis on the effects of essential oils in medicine today earned her the internship with the CDC."

Nita grinned. "I've used locally growing plants more than once in my life."

During the wee hours of the morning, when they talked all night long, she'd admitted to Daniel that she'd poisoned a target with what the locals thought was a weed.

"So, what did Chyna with a *y* suggest?" The snipe in Nita's comment caught Daniel's attention. He wondered why she didn't like the young woman, but the animosity was obvious.

"She advocated a tea made with elderberry and olive leaf." James turned his attention to Nita. "Did you know olive leaves contain oleuropein which disallows viral attachment to vigorous cells actually reducing the post, and concurrent, infection rate up to thirty percent?"

"That high?" Nita leaned her forearms on the table. "I had no idea. I'll have to add that to my herbal kit. Rosita, she's the household cook here, is already giving Bella elderberries, but I'll need to check with her on the other herbs. I was thinking of suggesting a little oregano. It'll help with respiratory tract disorders and gastrointestinal distress."

James smiled and pointed to the paper in front of him. "Those are on Chyna's list as well." He slid the paper over to Nita, completely bypassing Daniel as though he weren't even there. "These are the amounts she has suggested. Even though they are natural herbals, they still contain the basic compounds of modern medications, and we don't want to overdose her tiny little body."

Nita squeezed his hand. "Absolutely not."

Daniel smiled as he watched Simon and Santiago trot up the steps from the beach to the wide deck. His friend had been so helpful with the boy, not just since they had returned to Costa Rica, but while they had also been in camp. What would he have done without the man by his side for the past four years? Ti had always had his back. Briefly, he wondered what Ti was going to do when Daniel returned to the States.

In complete boy mode, Simon burst through one side of the double doors that led toward the ocean. He sprinted across the recreation room, Ti right on his heels. Both were laughing like children should.

"Boys," Rosita yelled from the swinging kitchen door. "And that includes you, Santiago Agustin Montoya. You know better. We walk in this house. Now go wash up. Supper will be served in five minutes."

Wow, Rosita had three-named Ti which meant she was serious.

"I'll take Simon upstairs to wash his hands." Daniel pushed his chair back from the table.

His friend scooped up Simon and was halfway up the steps when he called back, "You snooze, you lose." He gave the small child raspberries on his belly, making Simon giggle. "Besides, you look busy with important shit."

"Yeah, Daddy got important shit," Simon declared.

"You are such a bad influence on my son," Daniel accused.

"Yep, that's what favorite uncles are for." Santiago disappeared down the hall toward Simon's bedroom.

"Dr. Johnson, would you like to stay for supper with us?" There would be plenty of food for one extra.

The researcher gathered his papers. "Thank you, that's very kind of you, but we actually use our meal time as kind of a staff meeting. Each of us is taking a different approach to killing the virus and communicating in those clean suits is so cumbersome. We all have to eat, and five great minds together can accomplish more during a thirty-minute meal than any one of us could in days. Besides, the food at the hotel is absolutely divine. That cook over there is stupendous. Have you ever eaten over there?"

Nita slid Daniel a glance and a grin. Yes, he'd eaten over there many times. He and Uncle Tom had paid for the executive chef and sous chef to attend one of the most famous cooking schools in the world. A dessert chef would be joining the staff in a few months, as soon as she graduated and returned from Paris.

"The food is excellent," Nita agreed. Changing the subject, she continued, "You'll soon be getting some relief, perhaps as early as tonight." Nita stood when James did. "The CDC is sending additional scientists on the next flight down. I've been told everything you requested will be on that shipment as well."

James grinned ear to ear. "You are a guardian angel, Dr. Banks. I've never had support like this out in the field. Sure you don't want a job with the CDC?"

Nita shook her head. "No way in hell. I love my job. I'd never leave it."

A pang shot through Daniel. He wasn't sure why those words bothered him so much. He'd never thought about the future, least of all one with her. They were just good friends. True, friends with delightful benefits which he intended to explore even further just as soon as possible, but just friends. He understood that her job was extremely dangerous most of the time, but until that moment, it had never concerned him. Suddenly, the thought of life without Nita was incomprehensible.

As she walked James to the door, the older man placed a hand in the middle of her back. Daniel felt the need to claim her as his to let the world know she belonged to him. James was at least twenty-five years older than her and didn't seem to be Nita's type, but that didn't quell the alpha within Daniel.

He caught up with them in three long strides. "Dr. Johnson, I want to thank you for everything you're doing to help my daughter." He held out his hand.

As planned, James removed his hand from Nita's back to shake Daniel's. "We're not there yet, but I can assure you we are doing everything within our power to find a cure."

"Please, let me know if there is anything I can do for you." He opened the side door and pointed toward the path that would take him back to the hotel. "Have a nice evening, James."

When Daniel turned, Nita had her arms crossed under her nicely rounded breasts. "If I didn't know you better, I'd say you were jealous of James."

He glanced around and saw that no one was nearby. He gave her a quick kiss then placed his hand at her back to guide her toward the dining room table. "Maybe you don't know me as well as you thought you did."

She slid her arm around his waist then dropped her hand and smacked his ass. "Don't fall in love with me, Daniel Callahan. I'm not a good bet."

Reciprocating, he ran his hand down her back and cupped her rounded ass. "Then it's a good thing I'm only falling in lust with this body of yours that you so generously share with me." He leaned in closer and whispered in her ear. "Come to my room tonight. I want you in my bed the next time I take you."

The smell of food hit them before they heard the dishes being laid out on the buffet. As though a silent dinner bell had sounded, feminine voices filled the halls and the stairs.

Nita quickened her step and Daniel dropped his hand. He couldn't read the smirk she gave him. "I'll think about it."

Simon literally flew down the stairs, suspended in the air in Ti's strong hands, arms and legs outstretched. "Catch me, Daddy."

Daniel met them at the bottom, arms up, ready to take his son. "Thanks, Ti." Grabbing his son and automatically placing him on a hip, he laid a kiss on the small boy's forehead.

"No problem, bro." Ti glanced to where Nita was pulling out a chair next to Tori. "You were busy."

Damn. His friend was far too observant. He glanced toward Katlin to see if she had noticed any difference in the relationship between him and Nita. She was deep in conversation with Grace and hadn't seemed to even notice his presence.

Daniel went to his seat at the head of the table and slid Simon into the high chair next to him. Ti sat on the other side of his son.

"I've got the little man, you go through the line," Ti offered.

As soon as Daniel got up, he watched Ti peel a banana and share it with Simon. Damn it. Why hadn't Daniel thought of that? He was the child's father, yet once again, sucked at it. Santiago seemed to be a natural. But he had several brothers and sisters, older and younger. Many of them had children of their own, and Ti just took it all in stride. Now that Daniel was solely responsible for two little babies, he'd never been so scared in his life.

He stepped into line right behind his sister. "Did I see you go out today?"

"Yeah." Katlin scooped up a large portion of chicken smothered in chopped up fruit. Daniel decided he'd try some of that, too.

As she spooned what looked like purple potatoes onto a plate, she explained, "The researchers needed some healthy blood for their tests so USSOCOM arranged for us to meet two teams of SEALs and two teams of Special Forces back at the Honduran camp. I flew the jet over and back. It gave me a chance to work with Kayla, the other Black Swan team leader."

Daniel helped himself to a large portion of pasta. "So how are things going with you and Alex?" He really liked his sister's fiancé. It was quite a contrast to how much he really hated her first husband. Tyler Malone had been a douche bag of the highest degree. Although Daniel felt bad for his sister's loss, the world didn't lose much when that man was killed.

He looked at her empty left hand. The last time he'd seen Alex, Daniel had given him a large blue diamond that their father had brought back from Africa for their mother decades ago. "Is he ever going to make an honest woman out of you?"

She smiled over her shoulder at him. "We're getting married. I'm just not sure when. I don't know if I'll be here for lunch tomorrow say nothing about a specific date months in the future. But I'm putting you on notice big brother, you are walking me down the aisle."

"I don't see a diamond on that finger, though." Daniel stirred some kind of extra vegetables then decided to pass on those.

Katlin pulled out the titanium chain she wore around her neck that was practically hidden by her dog tags. She dangled a beautiful ring in front of him. He grabbed it to see what Alex had chosen for a setting. The blue diamond was flanked by two white diamonds.

"Very pretty." He let it drop so it could be seen on the outside of her black tank top. "Smart idea not to show that beautiful blue diamond off in public, especially in this part of the world."

She took the ring off the chain and slid it onto her finger, admiring it from moment. Without warning, she threw her arms around him. "Thank you for giving Alex this diamond. I know it was one of Mom's favorites."

Uncomfortable with such a public display of affection, he patted her back. "I certainly have no use for all those gems you insisted I take."

She released him, and they moved down the line, continuing to load the large plates. "You'll find the right woman someday, and settle down, and have even more kids." Katlin sounded more confident than Daniel felt.

"I've got my hands full with the two I already have." He decided to set the plate down then go back and get something to drink. "What woman in her right mind would ever want to marry me? Fuck, once I get back to the States, chances are I'll be unemployed."

"My fuck broken," Simon announced in a loud voice as he raised his cast so everybody could see it.

Laughter erupted from every adult at the table.

CHAPTER 15

NITA LAUGHED SO HARD TEARS RAN DOWN HER CHEEKS. Someone probably should chastise Simon for swearing, but that wasn't her job. The boy was going to hear a whole lot of adult words, given the crowd around the large dining room table.

Simon basked in the attention. It was obvious, at least to her, that the child had very little positive reinforcement in his life. He'd certainly had enough negative. She'd look into scar minimization the first chance she got. No child should wear the evidence of abuse all his life. Would he be embarrassed to go shirtless on the beach? As a teenager in a pickup basketball game, would he always choose to play on the shirts team rather than skins?

He was such a beautiful child. He would grow up handsome and strong like his father. Resisting those gorgeous blue-on-blue eyes would be difficult for any woman, but would Simon be able to find one who could see beyond the scars on his back? Would they define him as an adult? Would he all too often see the pity in feminine eyes every time he became emotionally close to a woman? When he took a lover, would he leave his shirt on so as not to deal with the questions?

Her heart broke for the boy's future.

Yeah, a woman would have to be crazy to take on Daniel Callahan and his premade family.

Glancing at his easy smile, well-defined jaw, and ripped body, he'd make any woman wet. And rightfully so. The man knew his way around a woman's body. He'd invited her for a repeat tonight, but she wasn't sure she wanted to take him up on his offer.

She was not into relationships of any kind, and certainly not interested in one with him. His baggage included a diaper bag and the second was a kid-sized rollie plastered with superheroes. She never wanted children of her own, certainly not someone else's. She preferred to deal with adults. At least they could tell her what hurt.

Straight white teeth gleamed at her. Daniel was too damn good-looking in a ruggedly wild way. As though he knew she was thinking about him, he looked right at her. His silvery blue eyes turned to heated sapphires filled with promise.

She'd occasionally gone back for seconds with the same man, especially when the first round had been exceptionally sweet. She hadn't tasted Daniel yet. She wondered how he'd take it if she offered to tie him up to that big four-poster bed of his. Nita tended to be on the dominant side, especially in bed. She was used to giving orders and having them instantly obeyed. With Daniel, it would be a fight of wills. Fuck, it would be fun.

"Is the clean room completely set up yet?" Santiago asked.

Nita slid back into the conversation, still undecided whether to join Daniel in the night. "We have more equipment that should arrive after midnight along with several more scientists so we can expedite the research." She went on to give everyone at the table an update.

Conversation ebbed and flowed, two or three occasionally breaking off into side discussions. Before she knew it, the meal was complete.

"I'm headed outside to talk to Alex for a while," Katlin announced as she refilled her wine glass.

"Hey, Tori and Lei Lu, want to get a nightcap with me over at the resort bar?" He danced his way to their end of the table, grabbing Lei Lu's hand and twirling her around. "After we tear up the floor for a while"—he pulled Tori to her feet and spun her into his arms—"you'll protect me from all those hungry female tourists, won't you?"

"Who's going to protect you from those two?" Nita found it interesting that Santiago hadn't asked her. Over the past year, they had often gone dancing together. True, it had usually been as a group, but he hadn't even looked her way tonight. Did he know about her and Daniel? Did the others?

She covertly scanned the crowd to see if anyone was acting strangely toward the two of them. Everyone seemed to be normal. Perhaps it was just her paranoia.

"Daniel, I'll be happy to go watch Bella for a few hours if you want to join Santiago and the others next door." Grace lifted Simon out of his highchair and planted him on her hip. "I can put this adorable little boy to bed for you."

The smile he gave her friend was genuine. "I truly appreciate the offer, but I think I'm going to call it an early night. I'll take the little man upstairs and read him a few books then shoo Kira back to the hotel. That woman has been a godsend watching over Bella. She needs a night off much more than I do." He glanced over his shoulder at Santiago. "I'm pretty sure there's enough of Ti to go around, and to keep all of you entertained."

"Hey, big guy," Tori planted fists on her hips and glared at Daniel. "I'm perfectly capable of finding my own entertainment for the night."

"You should invite team two," Grace suggested. "If they have the night off, they might enjoy hanging out with you guys."

Santiago spread his arms wide and gave a devilish smile. "More women for me. I like the sound of that."

Those headed out dancing decided to change their clothes and meet back in half an hour.

Nita passed Grace and Daniel on the way to the steps.

"*Mith* Nita, you read me a book?" Simon sounded so tired. He weakly reached out for her. "You read real good."

When the child looked at her with those puppy dog eyes, she couldn't say no. She took him in her arms and headed upstairs. "Are we reading books in English or Spanish tonight?"

He laid his tired head on her shoulder. "Just book. I like picture."

"I can take him," Daniel offered, climbing the steps beside her.

"I've got him." There was something so sweet and innocent about carrying a child to bed.

Daniel opened the door to Simon's room and helped him into pajamas and the nighttime pull-up diaper.

"I no pee the bed...*moth* time," Simon reassured Nita. "I'm a big boy."

After brushing his teeth, with a lot of help from his dad, Simon laid in the middle of the bed with stacks of books all around him.

"Whoa there, son." Daniel shuffled through them moving several over to the side. "One book. Ms. Nita will read just one book."

Simon picked up two books, seemingly at random and handed one to his father and one to Nita. "One book each." He gave her that adorable baby smile with all twenty tiny teeth.

"Damn, they learn early." Daniel took the proffered book and lay down on the bed next to Simon. Shrugging, Nita took the other book and lay on the boy's other side.

Thirty minutes later, and a second book read by each of them, Daniel stood. "That's all for tonight, son." He kissed the small child on his forehead.

The sight of their two heads, one large and the other so small, Daniel's black hair covering Simon's fine blond locks was a precious picture that instantly burned into her brain and onto her heart. Such a good man. Such a good boy.

"Night *kith, Mith* Nita." Simon ordered as he rolled toward her. She placed her lips on the softest skin she'd felt in years. Nothing was quite like a child's cheek. It was no wonder many mothers kiss their children so often. When she leaned back, she doubted Simon had received many maternal kisses. She didn't want to think about that anymore tonight.

"Sleep well, Simon." She rolled off the bed and headed out the door.

"Good night, son." Daniel's deep voice reverberated right behind her.

Her room was only a few steps across the hall, but before she reached for the handle, Daniel was right behind her.

With her back to him, he slapped one hand on each side of the door jamb. "I want you in my room in one hour."

The demand rankled Nita. No one ordered her around except a superior officer. And no one ordered her into their bedroom. "I don't see that happening."

Then he kissed her neck just below her ear. "And why is that?"

"Men don't order me into their bedroom, they..." She was having difficulty remembering why. He kissed his way down to her collarbone then pulled her top and bra strap off her shoulder replacing it with light kisses. She drew in a breath of air which helped clear her head. "They ask me. Some even beg."

"I've never begged a woman to go to bed with me." Daniel laid teeth gently on her shoulder.

"I'm not sure this is a good idea," she lied.

He kissed his way back up her neck and traced the outer shell of her ear with his tongue. "Nita, if you join me in my bed tonight, I can guarantee it will be unforgettable."

That certainly wasn't begging, nor was it a plea, although it was most unquestionably a promise. She could only imagine the things they would do tonight in his bedroom.

"Turn around," he commanded.

Ever so slowly, she turned to face him. She stared into those beautiful blue eyes, intensified by desire. "I want you, again, and again." He leaned his forehead to hers. "I can't explain why, but everything is different with you." He closed his eyes. "Give me about an hour to go through everything with Kira to make sure I know exactly what has to be done tonight for Bella." He opened his eyes, and it was as though he could see all the way through to her soul.

"I'll come check and see how the two of you are doing. That's the only promise I'm going to make." She refused to commit to anything more.

"I can promise that if you come to my room, you'll come so hard, you'll never regret it." He brushed his lips across hers and pushed himself off the door frame.

The view of his backside as he strolled toward the double doors at the end of the hall was enough to make her go wet.

Damn, what that man could do to her. The corners of her mouth kicked up. What that man would do to her.

One hour later, Nita softly knocked on Daniel's door. When he opened it, he scanned the entire length of the second floor.

Silly man, she'd already done that. Most of the others were at the resort, except for Katlin and Grace who were drinking wine out on the deck. Nita had even gone to the kitchen to retrieve a fresh bottle and slightly heated it for Bella.

Holding up the bottle, she asked, "Is Bella hungry yet?"

Daniel opened the door wide and gestured for her to walk in. As soon as she entered, he backed her up against it, but didn't touch her. "No, but I am."

"Banging against the door will certainly wake up the baby, and probably bring your sister and Grace running, weapons drawn." She shoved him out of the way, glancing at the sleeping baby in the crib.

She prayed that Bella wouldn't wake up while she was there. Feeling the need to check on the child, she lifted the file and scanned through the meticulously recorded details. Her fever was still going up and down, but it looked as though it wasn't spiking into the dangerous ranges.

"Kira takes her temperature every time she wakes up or every three hours, whichever comes first." Daniel pointed to the bag hanging on the nearby pole. "She said this should be more than enough to make it through the night."

Nita agreed. She set the bottle in the warmer next to the crib so it would be ready when Bella woke again. Nita couldn't bring herself to even touch the child. Fortunately, Daniel ran his hand through his daughter's blond hair and blew cool air over her scalp.

"Her fever is down right now, but Kira said we have to

watch for a spike in about three hours." He picked up a syringe. "I have to inject this into the tube here." He pointed to the correct spot.

He smiled. "Kira told me you were just down the hall, and if it was something I couldn't handle, to go get you." He stepped close but didn't move to touch her. "I've got something you need to handle."

She slapped his shoulder and scowled at him. "That is such a cheesy line."

"I'm serious," he declared.

One look in his eyes, and she saw he was serious. "What is it?"

"I don't want to leave Bella alone." He lifted his shirt away from his body. "But I haven't completely mastered dirty diapers, yet. I had to change her about ten minutes before you arrived." He looked down at his shirt and winced. "I have baby shit and throw up on me. Before I even get close to you, I want to shower."

Nita burst out laughing then quieted when the sound startled Bella. "I think I can handle this for a few minutes. I'd rather join you in the shower, but I'll simply wait for you here in the living room."

He flashed her one of those signature Daniel grins and kissed her quick. "I'll only be a few minutes."

"Go." She pointed toward the bathroom. "I'll make myself comfortable on the couch."

Picking up the chart on her way to the seating area, she studied it carefully this time. Without giving it a second thought, she pulled out her satellite phone and placed a call to the neonatal unit at Walter Reed Military Medical Center. Using the app on her phone, she ran some calculations. Medication doses were correct. She could see that Kira was being very careful with the amounts.

Nita never heard the shower go off, or Daniel walk out. When he brushed the curls off her face, she nearly jumped out of her skin. Lifting her eyes from the chart, her view was filled with Daniel's erect cock covered in a towel wrapped low around his waist. Unable to resist, she leaned forward and lifted the terrycloth. "Is this for me?"

"Most definitely." He glanced over at the crib twenty feet away along the far wall. "She'll be out for a few hours. I want you in my bed." Lifting her off the couch as though she weighed nothing, he carried her to his bedroom at the other end of the suite. He laid her on his turned-down bed and raked his gaze down her body. "You're wearing far too many clothes for this party." He grinned at the use of repeating her words from the last time they were together.

Curling his fingers at the hem, he pulled her shirt over her head, and quickly divested her of her bra. Staring for only a moment at her bared breasts, he took her shorts and underwear off her at the same time. She kicked and her sandals flew through the air.

While still standing, he lightly ran calloused fingers around the oval of her face, down her chest, ignoring her breasts, to cup her mound.

"Christ, you're beautiful." He leaned over and kissed her, thrusting his tongue into her mouth at the same time he separated her folds and dove into her sheath with his fingers.

The sudden dual assault nearly brought her to climax. She grabbed his shoulders and pulled him down onto the bed next to her. Now that he was within reach, she grabbed his cock and began stroking it up and down in rhythm with his tongue and fingers.

"Enough." Daniel reached into his nightstand, pulling out several condoms and tossing them on the dresser. "Don't worry, angel, there are more where those came from."

"You're pretty self-confident, aren't you?" She teased.

"Maybe you're right." He rolled back toward the nightstand. "I'd better grab some more."

She giggled. "If we use all those, I won't be able to walk tomorrow."

He rolled all the way back over on top of her spreading her legs with his knees. He ripped open the first packet and quickly rolled it on. "I can't wait any longer."

"No need to wait." She grabbed his cock and guided him inside her.

As he leaned on his forearms, he watched her with an intensity unlike any man ever had before. He ran his fingers through the curls on both sides of her face before he leaned in and kissed her, never missing a beat. She lifted her pelvis to meet his thrusts, faster and faster until she was ready to burst.

"Go ahead, angel, make us fly." His deep rumbling voice reverberating against her oversensitive nipples was all it took. She dug her fingernails into his bare back, clamping down on her scream so it came out as uncontrolled whimpers. His whole body stiffened as he shoved deep inside her.

Nita had vague recollections of him rolling slightly off to the side, pulling her with him. Her name was a whispered breath of hot air across her temple.

Water running in the bathroom revived her from the third orgasm of the night. Daniel was a voracious lover. It was as though he was starved for sex. He liked every position humans could have.

She heard a light cry from the crib located in the seating area of the suite.

Oh, fuck. Had they awakened Bella? Nita looked at the clock and realized it had been over three hours since she'd walked into his bedroom. She padded over to the crib and glanced in. Was it the nightlight making the baby look so red?

She flipped on the muted light over the changing table and saw that Bella's whole body was red. As she reached for the child, her stomach flipped over.

She was going to throw up.

Glancing toward the bathroom, then back at the baby, she fought for which to deal with first, the sick baby or her revolting stomach.

She had to do something right then. She had to act. The last thing she wanted was to lose another child. The last time her actions weren't the right ones. But losing a baby because she didn't act at all would be worse than making the wrong decision.

Bella opened her eyes and looked right at Nita as though begging for help.

Her heart beat so fast that blood rushed through her ears. She couldn't catch her breath as though invisible fists clamped around her lungs not allowing her enough oxygen.

But Bella needed her.

Now.

Fighting down the bile that threatened to spew forth, she snatched the child from the crib, grabbed the pole with the attached IV line, and sped toward the bathroom.

"Daniel, lay that towel down on the counter." Nita's mind and body had clicked into emergency mode. She shoved any memories of previous babies into a corner where they belonged.

"What's wr—" Daniel didn't bother with the rest of the words, he simply obeyed her orders. "Christ, she's so red." He touched his daughter and snatched his fingers away as though burned.

"Put a plug in the sink and fill it with lukewarm water. Not cold." Nita quickly stripped the one-piece sleeper off Bella and felt the waves of heat emitted from her body. That alone would help cool her down. Unfastening the tabs to her diaper, she saw it was soaked with almost brownish urine.

"Damn it," she said under her breath. "She's not getting enough liquids." Increasing the drip, she then checked the needle. If they didn't keep her hydrated they would start losing veins.

"How's this?" Daniel stuck his hand into the water.

Holding the baby onto the counter with one hand, Nita stuck her elbow into the sink. "Warm it up just a little bit. Too much temperature difference could put her into shock."

Daniel's eyes got huge, but he did as she requested. Retesting the water, she carefully slid the screaming baby into the sink.

Thank God they were on the far side of the house from most everyone else.

"Take over for me." Nita stepped aside so Daniel could move up next to the sink. She handed him a clean washcloth from the towel rack and demonstrated how to cool off her head. "I'll be right back. I just need to get the acetaminophen." At his questioning look she added, "Baby Tylenol."

It took nearly an hour for the medication, and impromptu bath, to bring her fever back down.

Daniel sat in the rocking chair with a towel wrapped around his hips and tried to feed her to no avail.

"Let me try," Nita, wrapped in a bath sheet, and Daniel switched places. "Was Bella breast-fed?"

"Yes. Both my children were." His lips went flat. "I don't think their mother did it out of any maternal instinct, but rather from laziness."

Nita teased the baby's mouth with the nipple on the bottle. Bella just wasn't interested. She tried changing to a different position with no luck.

Daniel continued, "It was easier for her to whip out a tit than bother making a bottle. She liked showing her tits to anyone who wanted to see them."

Nita looked up at him, aghast.

"Don't look so surprised." His gaze fell on his daughter. "Even though Cris gave her to me, she gave herself to several other men in camp, especially when she thought it would make me jealous or punish me." He chuckled. "I never really cared about her. I think somewhere in her sick little mind she believed that by having my babies, my love for my children would transfer to her. No way in hell was that ever going to happen."

"But you were obviously fucking her bareback. You know how dangerous that is," Nita chastised.

"I've never had sex without a condom." Daniel stared at her. "I swear to you. Looking back on it now, I think she actually sabotaged the condoms. In all my life, and I have a lot of sex, I've only ever had two condoms break. Both resulted in my children." He crossed his arms over his bare chest and leaned against the crib. "I don't believe in coincidences. To be honest with you, until they were born, I didn't believe either child was mine. But the minute I saw those Callahan eyes, I knew."

Nita changed position again, and Bella rooted around close to Nita's nipple. She suddenly remembered a technique one of the older nurses taught her on her neonatology rotation. She tucked Bella into the crook of her arm as though she were going to nurse her with her own breast, then slipped the bottle into her mouth.

Bella latched on and sucked. Nita's own bare breast pressed up against the baby's cheek, convincingly fooling her.

"Thank you, Jesus." Her prayer was heartfelt.

The infant twisted a little and laid her tiny hand on Nita's breast as though to hold it in the proper place. Her whole body covered in goosebumps. She'd never felt anything so perfect in her life. If anyone had asked Nita before that very instant about natural mothering instincts, she'd vehemently inform them that she had none, and never wanted any.

Holding Daniel's daughter in her arms, the child practically sucking on her breast, Nita decided she wanted this for herself...someday. She glanced up at Daniel who wore a contented smile as his daughter finished the bottle.

Nita's heart sank deeper.

CHAPTER 16

FOR NEARLY THREE DAYS, DANIEL HAD SEQUESTERED HIMSELF in his suite with his daughter. She'd fucking scared the shit out of him the night Nita had slept over. He'd never been so thankful for a good friend in his life. When she had dashed into the bathroom with Bella, ordering him around, telling him what to do to save his daughter's life...he'd never felt so useless.

Not wanting her out of his sight, Daniel had brought his baby downstairs with him when he and Nita had been summoned. And thank God for Nita. When she hadn't been in his room caring for the baby, she'd been in the clean room helping the scientists. Kira had also been a godsend, relieving him for short periods so he could spend a few quality hours with Simon, but USSOCOM had her out on missions every day in support of the researchers.

Dr. James Johnson, once again, sat nervously on the opposite side of the table from Nita and Daniel. From his pocket, he produced a small vial. "I feel confident our latest solution will help your daughter."

Daniel had prayed every night for a miracle. His beautiful

daughter couldn't seem to break the fever long enough for her body to fight the infection.

The doctor rambled on in scientific terms about how it worked, but he couldn't seem to use words with less than seven syllables. Exasperated, he finally said, "Whoa, James. Just cut to the chase. What do you need? More blood from Bella? You need me to go hunt down more survivors up north? Tell me in simple terms."

Nita put her hand on his forearm. "Thankfully, they don't need any more of Bella's blood. It worked on the latest samples we gave them. He needs your permission for human testing."

Well, hell. That was easy. He'd just go back to the encampment and roundup a dozen or so survivors, whatever he needed. "Sure. I'll leave within the hour and get you some volunteers."

Nita's fingers tightened. "No, what he's asking is if you will let him use this on Bella."

Fear shot straight to his balls. Make his baby a guinea pig? He automatically cradled Bella closer. "Is it dangerous?"

"I won't lie to you, Daniel." Nita reached over and caressed the baby's cheek with the back of her knuckles. "Any new drug is dangerous because we have no idea what side effects it might have. But I wouldn't suggest this if I didn't think it would help her. I've seen how positively the cells react to this medicine. It's almost a miracle. This combination seems to coat the healthy cells and repels the virus. The healthy cells then reproduce almost twice as fast as normal, as though they are pushing the infected cells out of the body."

He stared at one of the smartest women he knew and choked on his next question. "Is she going to die?" Heat and pressure built up behind his eyes, emptying teardrops that he quickly blinked away. He forced in a deep breath hoping to relieve the pressure from his chest while he waited for her answer.

"We're all doing everything in our power to make sure that doesn't happen." Nita's eyes glistened under the chandelier. "I love her, too," she added just above a whisper.

Daniel had watched the love grow between his children and Nita. Simon seemed to blossom under her affection and attention. Sure, she'd spent every night in his bed, but every few hours he'd awaken alone, and find Nita in the rocking chair with Bella snuggled against her bare breast. That wasn't a dedicated physician, that was a loving, caring woman. His woman was amazing.

"So, what you need? Do you have something I'm supposed to sign relieving you of any responsibility?" At this point, Daniel just wanted them to give her the shot, inject it into her IV, do whatever it took to make his baby better.

"No, just your permission." James handed the bottle over to Nita who pulled a syringe from her pocket.

It didn't seem like she put very much into the IV, but he trusted Nita completely.

"Let's get this little baby back to bed." Nita grabbed the pole and headed toward the stairs. She glanced over her shoulder. "James, I'll keep you posted hourly with her progress.

"Thank you, Dr. Banks. I'll see myself out." James stood and quickly left the house.

As soon as they had Bella settled back in her bed, he took Nita in his arms. "Angel, I think we should both take a nap."

"I need to check her every hour, but I could use a combat nap." He picked her up and placed her on his bed, then covered her, clothes and all.

"I'll take first watch," he promised and brushed a kiss

over her lips. As he crossed to the far end of his suite, he fully intended to let her sleep as long as she would. He set an alarm on his phone and stretched out on the couch with a magazine he'd been intending to read for over a year.

"Well, hello there pretty blue eyes," Nita's sing-song voice brought Daniel out of a deep sleep.

He filled the couch, armrest to armrest, and had a blanket over top of him. As he blinked awake, he realized a few lights were on and it was dark outside. Throwing off the blanket, he shot to the crib where Nita leaned over talking to his daughter.

"Why didn't you—" He started to chastise Nita then tiny noises caught his attention.

As soon as he looked at his child, she smiled up at him, moving her arms and legs all at the same time. She tried to roll over, but the board holding her arm straight for the IV kept getting in the way.

Nita picked her up and took her over to the changing table, talking to her constantly.

"I'm sorry, I guess I fell asleep." Daniel felt like a total idiot. "How long has she been awake?"

Stripping off the baby pajamas, Nita said in that same melodic voice, "This time, just a few minutes. I heard her over here cooing, so I thought I'd get her up and see if she can drink some more."

He noticed two empty bottles next to the warming tray. Holy fuck. How long had he slept? Checking his watch, he realized he zonked out for six hours. Christ, he was a horrible father. He'd promised Simon to take him fishing for an hour this afternoon. Well, one more failure in the father column. He'd also missed supper, but he knew Rosita would have left him plenty of food in the kitchen. She loved him like a son.

After changing Bella's diaper, Nita took her vitals then handed her to him. "Sit and give her this bottle."

Obeying, which was the least he could do since he'd abandoned her for hours, he sat in the rocker. Bella eagerly took the bottle, placing both hands on it as though she were the one holding it.

"I feel absolutely horrible that I fell asleep," he admitted to Nita.

She looked up from her clipboard. "Why do you think I was a bitch and left you on the couch?" Her smile told a different story. "Daniel, neither of us had much sleep in the last several nights. When we weren't fucking like bunnies, we were tending to Bella. The stress finally caught up to you. I made the executive decision to let you sleep. Hate me for it if you want, but it's done." She gave him an evil grin. "And now that you're fully rested, as soon as I give her this last dose, I'm going to my bed and sleep for the next eight hours."

Nita hung up the clipboard and went to him. "The antiviral is working perfectly. There doesn't seem to be any side effects. Every hour, she's becoming more and more responsive."

"Thank you, angel, for everything." Daniel gazed into Bella's bright eyes. He was amazed at the turnaround she'd made in just a few hours. He remembered Simon at that age. He was the cutest little kid. "What time did Rosita bring Simon back home, do you know?"

Nita's smile was warm. "He was half asleep after playing with her grandchildren all day. When you didn't make it down for supper, she came up here to check on you. She's the one who put the blanket on you. She dropped Simon off, and he fell asleep in your bed while I read him his stories. Once Bella fell back asleep, I carried him into his own bed and tucked him in." She yawned. "I'm out of here."

"Please, stay with me tonight."

She shook her head. "No. You've got this."

"I know I do." He looked into Nita's hazel eyes that seemed more brown this evening. "But I want you."

She grinned. "Daniel Callahan, you are the biggest horn dog I have ever met. You always want me, if not for my body, then for taking care of your baby." She leaned down and gave him a quick kiss. "I am going to go to bed. In my own room. And sleep. Alone." She then kissed Bella on the forehead.

She only got a few steps when she turned. "They're processing enough antiviral tonight for your encampment. I'll be heading up there tomorrow with my Black Swan team. You're welcome to come along. Now that Bella is feeling better, Rosita's daughter has volunteered to care for her for a few hours if you want to check in with your men. We've promised Uncle Tom not to break your cover. I'll see you in the morning at breakfast."

"If you stay, I promise you more orgasms," Daniel teased, but he could see just how tired she really was.

"Write this date on the wall, and let's hope we don't paint before it happens again, but I'm just too tired for a big O." She quietly closed the door behind her.

"Looks like it's just you and me for tonight." He lifted Bella to his shoulder and was quickly rewarded with a hearty belch. It was one of the best sounds he'd heard in days.

Santiago knocked shortly after daybreak. "We're headed for camp in thirty minutes. If you want to go with us, Maria will take care of Bella and Simon while we're gone."

"That would be awesome." Daniel had spent several summers and holidays at the Callahan compound, practically growing up with Rosita's family. He'd known Maria since they were both teenagers. Last year she'd left teaching kindergarten to have their fourth child and be a stay-at-home mom. Her son was only a few months older than Simon and the boys got along great. He felt confident that if she became overwhelmed, Rosita would jump in and help.

Both Kira and Nita followed Ti into the room where Daniel was attempting to take Bella out of her sleeper. She was so active this morning, grabbing at everything. His heart filled knowing his baby was getting better every minute.

"Looks like she drank well last night." Nita pointed toward the empty bottles.

"I'll check with Rosita to be sure she has more made before we go." Kira gathered the bottles and headed down stairs.

"Hold off on that a minute if you would, please," Nita asked as she flipped over the chart.

Daniel was so proud of himself for continuing to keep accurate statistics all night and recording them just as Kira and Nita had done for days.

"Kira, let's get this IV out of her. She's drinking enough fluids on her own now." Nita stood next to Daniel, acting completely professional. From looking at the two of them, no one would know that twenty-four hours ago he'd had her bent over the bed, taking her from behind, or any of the other positions they'd explored while sequestered in his suite for days.

Damn. He'd missed her so much last night. He'd gotten used to rolling over and snuggling into her, having her at his side comforting him as much as Bella. She'd been his rock through one of the worst times of his life, yet never made him feel bad about the things he didn't know. He'd started to believe that with her by his side, he could be a good father.

Last night had been good for him. He'd had to handle Bella completely on his own, and he'd done it. Fuck. He'd even changed the most disgusting smelling diaper on the planet. Dead bodies and rotting garbage smelled better than what came out of his little girl. But he'd handled it all on his own.

Nita was so close he could smell her body lotion. Yesterday, or maybe it was two days ago, he'd rubbed it over every inch of her body after their shower. She claimed it helped keep her olive skin soft and moist.

He hoped after they finished in the camp today, that she'd return to his room, and his bed. If the inoculations worked as well on everyone in the camp as they had on Bella, Nita would soon be leaving him. Her job there would be complete, and she'd be on to the next mission. It could be months before she was back in Costa Rica.

But that wouldn't matter. He had no idea where he'd be, but it wouldn't be in Nicaragua. Most likely, somewhere in the United States. Probably Washington D.C. He wondered if Katlin had rented out their parents' home in that area. She'd inherited most of the U.S. properties. He hadn't wanted them and refused to be responsible for property thousands of miles away while he was undercover.

Nita had been such a good friend to him, and he was going to miss her. They'd both known from the beginning that their relationship was purely sexual and temporary. He helplessly looked on as Nita and Kira worked on his daughter.

Simon came running into the room, looked up at all the adults, then wove through the bodies until he found his father. He threw his little arms around Daniel's legs. "Morning, Daddy. *Mith Rothita thay breakfath* ready, and you're holding everybody up,"

He picked up his son and gave him a huge hug. "I'm so sorry I fell asleep yesterday afternoon and missed taking you fishing. I promise I'll make it up to you. It just won't be today."

"I know." Simon planted a smacking kiss on his father's cheek. "You going to the camp. Can I go, too?"

"Time to move, boys and girls," Ti called and pretended to start shoving people through the door.

As Daniel carried Simon down the stairs to breakfast, he tried to explain, "There are a lot of people still very sick in camp, and we have to go take care of them. Maybe next time."

Three hours later, Daniel realized how true his statement had been to Simon.

On the way to camp, they passed through two villages where dead bodies lay bloated alongside the roads. Farm fields had been left unattended for so long weeds grew a foot tall in the tropical heat. Their miniature convoy of three Range Rovers seemed to be the only thing moving.

When Katlin had ordered everyone to go fully armed, Daniel had thought she was crazy. Sure, Nicaragua was never a safe place, but as they drove through jungles, he'd felt watched.

Pulling into the camp, the first person he saw was Doc. "Thank Christ you're here. I feared you had died. Please tell me you brought supplies."

Daniel grinned wide. "I did better than that, I brought the antivirus."

Doc threw his arms around Daniel and shook as though the man was crying. "So many. It took so many." He stepped back and regarded Daniel a moment. "The children?"

"They're both fine, now." Daniel took a deep breath. "It was touch and go with baby Bella for several days, but they figured out the right medication, and now she's better." He wasn't about to tell the man how and where his salvation came from, so instead, Daniel pointed to where the Ladies of Black Swan and Santiago were unloading cases of IV fluids and the antivirus.

Nita walked up carrying a tray of small bottles and a pack of syringes. "Good morning. I'm Dr. Banks. You have an infirmary established and perhaps triaged patients?"

"Did Cris become infected?" Daniel hadn't thought about the guerrilla leader in days.

"No. Well, yes." The doctor explained, "Cristobal suffered a very mild case early on. So did Emilio Bautista."

Good. At least Cris has one of his other lieutenants to protect him. For the first time, Daniel felt slightly guilty for grabbing his children and escaping to Costa Rica.

"And what of my men?" When he'd left, Hugo Vargas had been extremely sick.

"Some made it, others didn't." The doctor shrugged. "More than half are with Cris in San Miguelito. They left no guards here."

Cris probably figured they didn't need guards. With half the country sick and dying, fighting was the last thing on most people's minds.

"Doctor, if you'll show me the way, we'll get started," Nita pressed.

"Come with me." Doc sighed. "It isn't pretty or clean, like American clinics. But it's the best we can do."

Katlin walked up with a sniper rifle slung across her back and an M4 across the front. She had pistols on each thigh and, if Daniel had to bet, there were at least two other guns somewhere on her body.

"Does this camp not have any security?" she asked.

"We used to have layers of it, but Cris, Cristobal Maximo, isn't here. I guess he took what men were available with him to San Miguelito."

"Walk with me." She signaled for Tori, Lei Lu, and Grace to join her. "We'll establish a perimeter of security. Right now, that antivirus is more valuable than all the gold that can be mined from this country during the next century."

Daniel looked back over his shoulder in the direction where Nita and Doc had gone. He was pretty sure he knew where they had set up a makeshift hospital, but he wanted to know exactly where she was.

Santiago handed the last of the supplies to one of the healthy men and trotted up to their group. "What do you need me to do?"

"Help us establish a secure perimeter." Katlin had no authority over the man who had been their childhood friend, but he was willing to take orders from her.

"Go with them." Daniel glanced down the dusty excuse for a street. "I'm going to go guard the clinic. Like you said, sis, that antivirus is worth more than gold."

And Nita was priceless.

CHAPTER 17

"CRIS, IT'S VERY NICE TO MEET YOU." NITA SHOOK HANDS
with Cristobal Maximo, impressed with his excellent English,
which was only slightly accented. She then extended her hand
to the broad-shouldered bodyguard next to him. "Emilio, nice
to meet you, too."

She glanced over at the door where Daniel had stood
sentry for the past six hours. His relaxed posture told her a
lot. He obviously knew and trusted these men.

"Dr. Banks, I can't thank you enough for starting your
relief efforts with my camp. I apologize for not being here
when you arrived, but I had no idea you were coming." Cris
threw a glance toward Daniel as though blaming him.

Nita didn't like the accusation. "You can thank your
lieutenant for convincing the U.S. government to start in this
location. I'm sure you're aware that your entire country is
suffering from this epidemic. Managua was hit extremely hard."

She studied the men's reactions. Cris seemed almost
joyous at the information yet Emilio's lips flattened.

"Managua is no longer of consequence. General DeLeon

Cortez, the leader of our new government, is moving the capital to San Miguelito." Cris slapped Emilio on the back. "We've just returned from there, checking on the construction. This horrendous influenza has delayed our projects by several weeks."

Daniel turned so Nita could see him as he shook his head ever so slightly. They'd been ordered not to use the word Ebola in an attempt to keep a lid on the exact cause of the epidemic. If they could keep the truth contained within the borders of Nicaragua, continuing the guise of restoring order under the new government, hopefully worldwide panic could be averted.

Nita gave Cris an encouraging smile. "I'll check with my superiors and see if perhaps we can go to San Miguelito next."

That seemed to appease the camp leader. "That would be wonderful. The sooner we can start construction on the canal, the sooner my country can literally dig itself out of the sixteenth century and move onto becoming a prosperous, First World country."

Those seemed like lofty goals, but Panama had become a world power the moment the last canal lock released its water and the first ships successfully sailed away after traversing Central America. It could happen for Nicaragua within five years.

"Well, if you'll excuse me, gentlemen, I still have patients to attend to." Her gaze swept over the stinking room where men and women continued to lose bodily fluids. Now, though, lifesaving liquids, laced with antiviral medication, flowed freely into veins at every bed.

She was halfway down the second row of packed cots when Katlin strode into the clinic. "Now that Cris has returned with his security contingent, we're heading back home. Can you be ready in five?"

Nita glanced around at the sixty or more patients who needed her help. She'd ordered the camp doc to get some rest. Poor man. He'd been dealing with hundreds of patients, practically by himself, for days.

"You guys go ahead. I'm going to stay here tonight." She glanced around the room. When she caught Daniel's eye, she signaled for him to come over. "Is there somewhere I could sleep here tonight?"

"Sure. I'll show you to my tent." He held her gaze. "It's nowhere near as comfortable as the beds back at the Callahan compound."

She read his double meaning. "Bella is doing much better. You've got that handled." She tilted her head toward Katlin. "Besides, you have a house filled with women who rarely get to play with babies. I'm sure one of them can take care of her while you shower." Realizing she may have given away their intimate relationship, she added, "Or do whatever it is you do at night."

Katlin beamed. "I'd love some time with my niece." She looked toward Daniel. "Show Nita where to sleep and meet us at the Rovers in five."

"You're pretty bossy for a little sister," he chided.

"I'm wearing more guns than you. Get a move on." She was halfway to the door and turned around. "Nita, you sure about this?"

She knew what her friend was asking. All the Ladies of Black Swan were highly trained, special operatives. They were only left alone when they were undercover. Even then, they were monitored via hidden cameras planted everywhere, but they hadn't brought their favorite electronics on this mission. This was supposed to be a non-hostile environment in that Nita was not surrounded by tangoes. She was well-armed, and lethal even without weapons. She'd be fine for one night.

"I'm sure. I'll see you guys tomorrow."

After a confident nod from Nita, Katlin left.

"Come on." Daniel took Nita by the elbow. Tingles emanated from that point throughout her entire body, lighting up at his touch. "I'll show you where you can sleep."

The tents got larger and considerably nicer as they walked down the dusty row. Two distinct feminine giggles could be heard from the largest tent as well as a low male voice. From the tent on the right, a bed creaked rhythmically as a woman cried out in Spanish, "Harder, Emilio. I like the way you fuck me."

Daniel looked down at her with unspoken questions in his eyes. She took pity on him and answered in Spanish. "I'm fluent in several Spanish dialects, and you already know I'm good at pillow talk."

"I haven't taken part in the welcome home rituals in years." He looked contrite. "I had to when I first got here. I had to become one of them in every way. Then Cris gave me his sister. After that, many of the women in camp believed I was married and faithful to my children's mother."

Nita schooled her face, refusing to judge him for fear she'd be judged for the many things she'd done in the name of the mission. When she was home, she had a lot of sex. She liked sex. More than once she'd been told that she had a very male attitude toward sex. It had never mattered until she and Daniel had spent a celibate night together. Being there in camp, where Daniel had lived for several years with Bella and Simon's mother, she suddenly felt like the other woman. A dirty little secret that he'd sneak off to spend time with.

"My place is on the left." Daniel steered her toward the

tent and held open the flap. Stepping in behind her, he spun her around. Cupping her face with his big hands, he crashed his mouth on hers. His kiss was filled with heat as he dropped his hand down her back to grab her bottom and pressed her against him.

"Christ, I've wanted to do that for hours." Daniel touched his forehead to hers. "I'm sorry I can't stay here with you, but I real—"

"You need to get back to your children," Nita finished for him. She stepped from his embrace and glanced around the twelve-foot square tent. She thought it was a little odd that there was only a single cot, a sparse nightstand with a battery-operated lamp on top, a military style footlocker, and an extra pair of combat boots tucked under the bed.

Glancing over her shoulder at him, she asked, "Is this where you lived when you were on duty?"

Out of the corner of her eye, she watched him take in the tent. "No. I've lived here for over four years."

She turned to face him. "Where did the children live?"

"With their mother." As though a light bulb went off in his head, Daniel explained, "All the women and children live in the center of camp. It was safer for them, and easier to take care of the children in one location. The kitchen and bath house is there, a courtyard of sorts for them to play, and several small concrete houses."

"So you had one of the houses down there?" Nita pointed toward the center of camp.

"No, this is my place. My family lived down there." Defensively he added, "I saw my children...almost daily. At least I tried to."

Nita's jaw dropped. "You mean to tell me that you never spent the night with your kids until you brought them to me?"

Daniel spread his legs and fisted his hands on his hips.

"This is a very different culture from the United States. The women raise their children here while the fathers defend the camps and villages." He lowered his voice. "I did what I had to do to fit in. I did everything that was expected of a man in my position in this camp. That obviously offends you, but it doesn't mean I love my children any less than an American soldier who has to leave his family on a regular basis. Just because we don't live under the same roof like families do in the United States, it doesn't mean I don't love Bella and Simon." He threw his hands in the air. "The women wouldn't let me take care of my kids even if I tried. That's their way. It's just different here."

Nita suddenly realized the learning curve Daniel had climbed and conquered in just a few short days, all while worrying over a sick baby. The social structure in this area was not that different from other places around the world. In many countries, the women were the sole caregivers until the child reached a specified age. In some, at a given age, a boy is then turned over to his father for training on how to be a man. In many cultures, little girls rarely see their fathers.

What Daniel had done was nothing short of amazing. He'd taken on fatherhood and succeeded. She walked back to him and slid her arms around his waist.

"I do understand." She went up on tiptoes and placed a quick kiss on his lips. "And I understand you." She gave him one more kiss then smacked his butt. "You need to go. Give Simon and Bella a kiss good night for me, please."

He didn't let go. Instead he pulled her to him tighter. The kiss he gave her was a scorcher, deep and sultry. "That's to remind you what you're going to be missing tonight." He swatted her ass and left.

Seconds later, she heard Daniel talking with someone a few feet away. All she caught were few words. "Look after her for me," and, "she's special." At the last words, warmth swelled within her.

Nita was back in the tent six hours later. About four hours ago, shortly after dark, someone had brought her a bowl of rice and vegetables with some kind of meat mixed in. Other than sitting to scarf down that modicum of food, she'd been on her feet since arriving twelve hours ago. She was so tired, she couldn't sleep, so she lay on top of her lightweight bag thinking about Daniel. Mentally, she kicked herself for not leaving her satellite phone outside so the solar batteries could recharge. At least then she could have called or texted Daniel, just to hear from him one more time that night.

She heard men whispering outside her tent before someone knocked on the center pole. Thankfully, she'd remained dressed, so all she had to do was slide into her work boots and grab a gun.

"Who is it?" she called as she untied the inner flaps.

"Ma'am, it's Emilio Bautista. Daniel introduced us earlier today."

She remembered the man as being Cris's bodyguard. "Is there a problem in the clinic?" Or perhaps someone had been hurt.

"No, ma'am. Everything is okay in the clinic. Can you please come out?" She finished untying the flaps and stepped out. Something didn't feel quite right, so Nita put her fist on her right hip so it was close to the gun she had shoved in the back of her pants.

In the light of the half moon, Emilio seemed nervous. He kept glancing back at Cris's tent. Finally he spoke. "Daniel called and said you are to bring all the remaining supplies with you. He told me where to take you." He quickly added, "He will meet us there." Not once did the man look at her.

His gaze darted from tent to tent then down the road toward the clinic.

Emilio didn't seem this nervous earlier, but he may have been putting on a strong front in front of the other men. Daniel's and Cris's mere presence was formidable. Then, too, he was talking with a strange woman in the middle of the night.

"Where exactly are we going?" Nita asked in Spanish.

His eyes widened as though surprised she could speak the language. He replied in Spanish, "Daniel told me where to take you. He will meet us there."

She nodded. "Let me grab my things. Can you load the supplies we will need?"

Seemingly happier, Emilio nodded his head. "Already packed in the Jeep. You grab your bags. I'll wait here."

Repacking took only seconds. Before she threw the satellite phone in the bag, she checked it one more time, hoping for even one bar of battery left so she could shoot a message off to Daniel or someone on her team. Nothing. Damn. It was just a courtesy anyway. Her team knew exactly how to find her anywhere in the world.

She'd see them soon enough. Where, she had no idea. She slid her bag over her shoulder after moving another pistol to an out-of-pocket so it would be easy to reach. Stepping out, she was met not only by Emilio, but by two other men who were heavily armed.

"This way." Emilio pointed "We need to be very quiet. The whole camp is asleep, and we don't want to wake anyone up."

That was understandable, so Nita said nothing as they made their way to several military-looking vehicles. From the stack of boxes in the back, she worried that none had been left for the camp. Perhaps the original plan had changed so that the remaining supplies from that day would be moved forward, and the supplies coming in tomorrow would replenish Cris's camp. Or was it today? She glanced at her watch and saw that it was nearly two in the morning.

She sighed as she climbed into the backseat of the Jeep. It was going to be a long night. As they pulled out of camp, she noticed that they turned west on a dirt road and bumped along for about twenty miles before turning north on a relatively paved highway. The rocking of the Jeep lulled her to sleep.

She woke just as dawn broke. They were headed west again. "How much longer until we reach our destination?"

"It was good that you slept," Emilio said from the shotgun position. "You're going to have a full day ahead of you."

"What time will the other relief workers arrive?" she asked, holding with their cover.

The man next to her smiled showing several missing teeth. "No one is coming to help you."

Nita's blood ran cold. She pasted on a smile and stayed in character. "You mean no one is coming to help me *today*, right? Surely they'll be able to send more supplies and helpers tomorrow."

The man beside her chuckled then said in Spanish, "She's pretty, but not very smart. She'll still be fun to fuck."

Ice ran through Nita's veins. Damn, she hated being duped. If she hadn't gotten caught up in her work, she would've remembered to recharge the batteries on the sat phone. Bad Teeth beside her would never get the chance to even touch her. She'd kill every man in that vehicle before she'd allow them to touch her body.

"I'll bet she fights like a cat," the driver said over his shoulder. "I think I'll take her from behind so she can't dig those claws into me."

Oh, yeah. These guys were dead men.

"You idiots," Emilio yelled. "She speaks Spanish as well as you do and now she knows that no one is coming to save her. We need her. She has to make our men better."

Well, at least Emilio wasn't as stupid as he looked.

He turned in his seat so he could face her. "Dr. Banks, I promise you I will protect you from these savages, and any others who try to harm you. We need your help. Yes, I've kidnapped you, but if you make our men better like you did those back in camp, I promise you I will let you go free."

"Emilio, all you had to do was ask." Time to play good little woman doctor until she found the right opportunity to either kill them or escape. She wasn't really worried. Her team knew exactly where she was, even though she didn't have a clue. "We have more supplies coming into camp today. We'd already planned to go to San Miguelito next, and take care of the workers there for you."

"Exactly the problem," Emilio spat out. "That's why I need you to make my men better first."

"But aren't your men in San Miguelito?" Nita was getting very confused.

"No. My men took over the dormitories at the university in Managua, the true capital of Nicaragua. Then they all became sick with this horrific influenza. Many have already died." He jabbed a finger at her. "But you're going to make the rest of my men better."

"You keep saying *your* men. Who exactly are your men?" She needed to nail down as many details as possible. Was the man insane?

Emilio gestured to the men in the car. "We are members of the presidential guard forced undercover to keep an eye on that fool, Cristobal Maximo. As soon as my men are healthy enough, we are going to free the true president from prison and return Nicaragua to its rightful leadership."

"I'm going to help you," she lied. "How many men will I be attending to today?"

"About two hundred fifty are still alive, plus the fifty that didn't seem affected." Emilio simply stared at her.

"I can't handle that many patients by myself," she blurted out before she could engage the filter that rarely worked.

"You'd better figure out a way to." He tilted his head toward Bad Teeth beside her. "Maybe an hour alone with Franco would help you find the right motivation."

Oh. Hell. No.

CHAPTER 18

DANIEL COULDN'T WAIT TO SEE NITA, SO HE'D LEFT AS SOON as Maria had arrived that morning to babysit for him. He was delighted by his newfound fathering skills. Both children were ready—up, fed, dressed, the diaper bag was packed, and Simon even had four changes of clothes and a bathing suit in his very own duffel—by the time she and Santiago arrived. He was pleased at how smoothly everything had gone last night, too.

When he'd returned from the camp, he'd taken Bella outside to play in the crystal blue Caribbean Sea with him and Simon. After a delicious supper filled with lively conversation with his sister and the other members of her team, he'd bathed both children. For half an hour, they lay as a family on Simon's bed while Daniel read books to them before tucking in his son and kissing him good night. He even gave his son the extra kiss good night from Nita.

As he closed the door to Simon's room, he remembered his father doing the same thing for him as a child. Daniel smiled. He was doing the best he could to give his own children a good life...the same as his father had done for him.

Maybe his old man hadn't been the uncaring son-of-a-bitch he'd always thought.

Bella had slept through most of the night with only a three o'clock snack. She'd awakened such a happy child. Christ, he loved his children.

With every mile down the deeply-rutted road closer to camp, the more excited he got about seeing Nita. He hadn't been the only one to miss her last night. Simon had asked for her at bedtime. It nearly broke Daniel's heart to tell him that Nita wasn't there, and he wasn't sure when she was coming back. He wanted her lying on the other side of Simon every night as they read books to the children. Their children. And he wanted to fill that bed with more siblings for Simon and Bella.

As he crawled between the sheets, alone for the second time in as many nights, he missed snuggling into her even more than he missed sliding into her warm wet body. In the wee hours of the morning, while rocking Bella and feeding her a bottle, Daniel had been hit with the realization that he loved Nita. He'd loved her as a friend, he loved being her lover, he loved watching her with his children, and he loved that amazing woman. He couldn't imagine living the rest of his life without her.

He pressed on the accelerator to get to her faster. He needed to tell her exactly how he felt. At thirty-eight years old, he didn't want to waste any more time. His entire life was changing for the better. Soon, he'd be returning to the United States, and he wanted to make a home for the four of them.

Daniel just hoped Nita wanted the same thing.

The midmorning sun was already stifling hot as he made his way to the clinic, and the woman he loved. He was a bit surprised not to see Emilio at the door since he'd asked his fellow lieutenant to keep an eye on Nita in his absence. Perhaps the man had just taken a break.

"Hey, Doc," Daniel called as he stepped into the reeking crowded room. "Where's Nita?"

"That's what I'd like to know," the man snarled. "I had the night shift, and expected her to relieve me almost two hours ago."

Unease set into Daniel's every pore. It wasn't like Nita to shirk her duties. "I'll go find her."

Jogging to his tent, he asked everyone he encountered if they had seen the American woman doctor. Every inquiry was answered with a resounding no.

Finding his tent flap untied was not a good sign. As he stood in the empty space he had called home for far too many years, fear began to set in. There was no trace she'd ever been there.

He spun and tore out of the tent, about to rip Emilio a new asshole if he'd dared to leave Nita alone and something had happened to her. He didn't bother knocking on the tent pole, before he lifted the flap.

He was rocked back by the sight. All the personal items that had littered every surface were gone. Not a single picture of Emilio's parents, sisters and their families, or high school friends. Everything was gone. The battered green footlocker that lived at the end of the single bed was also missing. Emilio Bautista was gone.

At the creak of the Cris's double bed springs, Daniel knocked on the tent pole. "Hey, Cris. Did you know Emilio left?"

"He's probably just in the head," the camp boss said around a yawn.

"Cris, the man is *gone*." Daniel emphasized the last word.

The tent flap opened wide exposing Cris in nothing but a

pair of silk boxer shorts. Daniel was thankful the man at least covered his junk. It wasn't unusual for many of the men to walk out naked to take a piss first thing in the morning. After only a few nights at the Callahan compound living in luxurious civility, Daniel couldn't wait to leave this job. Camping would never be a family activity as far as he was concerned.

Cris scratched the hairs on his chest and yawned again. "What the fuck do you mean Emilio is gone? We put a hard dent in a bottle of eighteen-year-old Scotch together last night." He stretched and looked at the morning sun. "I haven't slept like that in years, especially without a woman in my bed." He rubbed his forehead. "Christ, I've got one motherfucker of a hangover. I didn't think I drank anywhere near that much."

Both men glanced at the half-filled bottle of scotch on the table between the two camp chairs.

"I think you were drugged." Daniel started putting together a plausible scenario, one he didn't like in the least. "Did you hear anything at all last night? Did you hear Nita screaming out? Any kind of a struggle?"

Concern covered Chris's face. "Nita? You mean Dr. Banks isn't here?"

"No. And all of her stuff is gone." Daniel thought he was going to revisit his breakfast.

Santiago came jogging up. "Katlin sent me to find you. All the medicine we left here last night is gone."

"What the fuck are you saying?" Cris snapped. "You think Emilio did this?"

"Nita is gone," Daniel said through clenched teeth. "So is Emilio."

"So are all the drugs needed to make the people in this camp better," Santiago added.

"We have to find her, now." Daniel ignored the other two men and headed to find his sister. "Ti, go find the guards who were on duty last night. Find out what they know."

"I'm on it." Ti took off in the opposite direction.

Where the fuck would that son of a bitch have taken her? The why was easy. Nita was the only one who knew how much, and how often, to give the antiviral medication. They needed the bags of fluid to rehydrate…someone. But who?

Daniel tamped down the panic that wanted to overtake his clear thinking. He found Katlin helping Doc inventory the few medical supplies they'd moved into the clinic last night for easier access.

"I think Nita was kidnapped." At Daniel's announcement, both his sister and the camp doctor looked up at him. "She's not in my tent, and Emilio Bautista is gone." Daniel shook his head. "I trusted that man to watch out for her, to make sure nothing happened to her. Fuck me. I practically gave her to him. Does she carry a tracking device of any kind?"

Katlin glanced at Doc. "We might be able to track her phone."

Daniel knew that was a lie. The EMP had obliterated most of the cell phone towers in the country through a weird system that was meant to divert calls to the next closest tower should one be hit by lightning.

As soon as they were outside, his sister tapped her ear. "Lei Lu, bring the toys and meet me at the Rovers. Black Swan team one, extraction point alpha, now."

He hadn't noticed the tiny comm unit that was molded in her ear. It was obviously custom-made. He wondered briefly if he'd been out of the loop so long that technology had leaped that far, or if his sister's team was allotted the latest and greatest technology.

When he and Katlin reached the three Land Rovers, Lei Lu had her laptop open and was attaching a thick antenna.

"Who do we need first, Lady Hawk?" Lei Lu clicked keys and the Black Swan logo appeared on the screen.

"We believe Nita has been kidnapped. Find her." Katlin stood to the side and let her teammate work. Daniel had no problem watching the screen. A graphic of the world popped up and rotated. Their location was indicated with a red dot. Satellites appeared as scattered as stars moving above the earth. Yellow dotted lines began connecting those dots. Some turned solid as a satellite picture of Central America began enlarging. In less than a minute, a green dot pulsed near Managua. A series of numbers ran along the bottom of the screen.

"Lady Harrier is just west of Managua," Lei Lu announced. "Her heart rate is normal at fifty-eight beats per minute, and her temperature is 99.1 which is within normal range for her."

"She doesn't seem under duress, so that's good." Katlin touched Daniel's bicep. "Lady Kite, expand and turn on infrared."

The long rectangular building burst with bright red. As Lei Lu expanded the view, it became obvious that Nita was in some kind of a barracks or dormitory, possibly a hotel. Some of the bodies surrounding her were much hotter than hers.

"Looks like they've converted the university into a hospital," Santiago said from behind them. "The men on duty reported that Emilio and two other men, the guys who arrived in camp the same time he did about two years ago, left in the middle of the night in one of the Jeeps after loading it with supplies. Both men confirmed that she did not leave at gunpoint. It seemed to them that she got into the Jeep willingly."

"Thank you, Ti. I appreciate that." Katlin gave their longtime friend a warm smile before turning to Lei Lu. "We've got to call this in. Get the general on the line. He might as well go ahead and call Uncle Tom at the same time. He may have another asset in place somewhere in Managua that we can tap."

The screen split with Tom on the left and General Lyon on the right.

"What's up ladies? This is coming across as a priority red." The general rocked forward and his chair squealed in pain.

"Lady Harrier has been kidnapped. We have located her two miles west of Managua in what used to be the university." Katlin's report was succinct. "We believe Emilio Bautista and two other men took her from the encampment where she was providing medical aid. They also stole the antivirus and other medications. Request permission for rescue mission."

"Permission granted." The general signaled to someone off screen. "What do you need?"

"The Black Swan team two helicopter. Their assistance would also be appreciated." Daniel loved when Katlin was in full Lady Hawk command mode. His sister was a kick-ass-take-names woman. So was Nita.

"Done." The general nodded to the unseen person next to him. "What else?"

Katlin glanced directly at Daniel. "Permission to hire local mercenaries."

"Daniel could be a great asset," Tom interjected.

"I want Santiago at my side," Daniel insisted.

"I'm going, too."

Everyone turned to see Cristobal Maximo dressed as the guerrilla leader he'd been for the past several years. Cris looked pissed dressed head to toe in camouflage with weapons strapped to both thighs and an M4 rifle casually slung across his chest. "These were my men. They fooled me, betrayed me, and abused my trust. No one gets away with that…and lives."

The general seemed to contemplate the situation for a long moment. "On the suggestion of the deputy director of the CIA, the two mercenaries are officially on the U.S. payroll. You have permission to give Mr. Cristobal Maximo, the Minister of Transport and Infrastructure in the new Nicaraguan government, a ride to Managua. I am required by the agreement with the new Nicaraguan government to inform General DeLeon Cortez of this rescue attempt. Anything that happens beyond casualties that may occur during the rescue, will be solely the responsibility of the new Nicaraguan government." The general reached to click his mouse but hesitated. Then he smiled. "Give General Cortez my regards. CO USSOCOM out."

That half of the screen went blank.

Uncle Tom's face filled the screen. "I'm sorry, but you took our primary asset in Managua to San Miguelito a few days ago. Our only other asset in that area was shot and killed two days ago. He had what he considered reliable intel that someone was putting together an army, and they were going to try to free the former president. There's still a very strong following of the overthrown regime in and around Managua. That's all I know at this time."

"Thanks, Uncle Tom. That's more than we had. We'll check back in later. Black Swan out." Katlin turned to face the three women and three men. "Any brilliant ideas on how we get Lady Harrier out of there?"

Lei Lu had watched Lady Harrier's movements all afternoon. She'd worked steadily moving from bed-to-bed, but no one seemed to interfere with her duties. To their surprise, no one even seemed to approach her. They had watched and timed the exterior guards, identifying patterns. An attempt to count the bodies had failed because the heat signatures were not always easily separated. There were three floors of patients, and only one Nita. Daniel could imagine how exhausted she was already, and would be even more so before she was rescued.

As Daniel wrapped his boots around the thick rope and grabbed on with both gloved hands, he peered over the edge of the jet black helicopter. The downwash felt like a huge hand trying to shove him out of the chopper and straight into an abyss. He hadn't fast roped out of the chopper in ten years.

Katlin cracked several chemical luminaries, shook them, and tossed them out. They scattered across the roof providing a visible destination. "You ready, big brother?"

"Yeah." Why the fuck had he volunteered to take point? Nita. That's why. He wanted to be the first to get to her. To save her, and bring her home.

Kira, acting as crew chief, smacked him on the shoulder. He shoved off from the chopper deck and let the rope slide through his hands and feet until he hit the roof then peeled off, making room for the next person.

He tapped down his night vision goggles and took a second to orient himself. The roof access was exactly where he expected it to be so he headed in that direction on quiet feet. He was shocked as hell when he discovered it unlocked.

"Lady Harrier is on the second floor," the feminine voice in his ear informed him and everyone else on this mission. He thought it was Mia, one of the team two Black Swans, but he'd only met them once.

"Roger that." He carefully cracked the door open and peeked down the steps. At his signal, Katlin stepped around him and headed down the first flight. They leapfrogged down to the second floor. He had insisted on going through the door first, so his sister was the one who opened it and peeked in.

"Alpha team, hold." The orders came through clearly.

Over his comm unit he heard grunts. "Guard was early. Handled. Lady Falcon moving to designated position." Daniel easily recognized Tori's voice. As the team's sniper she'd remained on the roof to cover their extraction.

"Alpha team, clear to move. You're going to have to search each room. The heat signatures from the different floors are blending."

At his sister's nod, she opened the door wide. He slid in and went to the right as planned. Lady Kite was immediately behind him and went left. Katlin remained to guard the door and cover the stairwell.

"Shit. The dead tango was just discovered. Guards are on third level searching for the intruders." The woman working control remained cool but urgent.

Daniel swept each room down the right side of the hall as fast as he could. He was so tempted just to yell out Nita's name and deal with any tangoes who dared stick their head out. The best rescue missions are the ones done silently and the kidnapped victim isn't missed until the team is long gone.

"Lady Hawk, tangoes are in the stairwell and headed your way," control center announced.

"On it," Lady Hawk said just above a whisper.

A slight worry ran through Daniel, but he was confident his sister could handle two tangoes. He was barely conscious of the scuffle and grunts transmitted to his comm as he hurriedly moved room-to-room.

Breathing only slightly faster than normal, his sister reported in. "Two more tangoes down. Lady Hawk returning to position."

He let out a slow breath of relief that his sister was uninjured. As he prepared to exit the room he'd just cleared, a door banged open at the far end of the hall. He could see Lei Lu in the open doorway across from him, out of sight from anyone else. They both froze in place.

"Dr. Banks, where are you?" the man bellowed.

Daniel recognized Emilio Bautista's voice.

"You need to keep it down," Nita chastised as she stepped out from the room two doors down.

Damn it. All they needed was another minute and they would've had her and been gone. *Fuck. Fuck. Fuck.*

"These men need their sleep if you expect them to get better." Nita's tone was low but stern. "What's wrong?"

She didn't sound distressed. Had she come there by choice?

"You need to come with me," Bautista insisted.

"No, I need to add the second dosage to the men on this floor, then I'll go with you," she argued.

The distinct slide of metal-on-metal echoed down the hall as a round was chambered into a gun.

Daniel didn't think. He drew his weapon and stepped into the hall. He was not going to let anyone take Nita from him. All he had to do was make sure she didn't get caught in the crossfire.

"Dr. Banks, you will come with me, now." Bautista could insist all he wanted, but Nita wasn't going anywhere with him.

"Emilio, don't you touch her. I have a thousand reasons to kill you," Daniel warned. "One for every minute she was your captive."

"Daniel, my friend, I needed her more than they did back in that disgusting camp. Those people were nothing. My men need to get healthy so we can free the president and restore peace and order to Nicaragua." Bautista was breathing hard and getting louder with every sentence. "You didn't really believe that bullshit that Cristobal Maximo spewed every night in a drunken stupor. General Cortez is an idiot. He'll run this country into bankruptcy within a year trying to build a new capitol and that foolish canal."

What the hell is that woman doing? Nita had been cleverly moving closer to Bautista while his attention was on Daniel and politics.

"Daniel, you're an intelligent man, you must see how impor—"

Nita lashed out with a roundhouse kick knocking the gun out of Emilio's hand. She stepped into his body grabbing his extended arm then kneeled, flipping the man over her shoulder onto his back. She used her elbow to smack the side of his head, rendering him unconscious.

The doors at both ends of the hall flew open. Katlin rushed in from behind Daniel as Cris barged in the same way Emilio had entered.

Nita stood, surveyed her handiwork lying cataleptic on the floor, then strode to Daniel and threw her arms around his neck.

He holstered his gun so he could wrap his arms around the woman he loved. "Don't ever do that to me again. I thought I'd lost you."

"Can't lose something you don't have. What makes you think you have me?" The glint in her eye gave her away.

"Oh, you're mine whether you admit it or not." He had to tell her how he felt. He couldn't hold it in any longer. "I love you, Nita. And that's never going to change." He squeezed her, never wanting to let her go. "Please, tell me I'm not alone in this."

"Well, I have to tell you that I've already lost my heart to somebody else."

Daniel stepped away and held her by her shoulders. "Who?" How could she have made love to him the way they had, yet been in love with someone else?

Nita visibly fought to withhold her feelings. "I have someone special waiting for me. Well, actually, there are two special people waiting for me...back in Costa Rica." She cupped his face and ran her thumbs over his cheekbones. "They both have your damnable blue Callahan eyes." She went up on tiptoes and gave him the briefest of kisses. "I fell in love with Simon and Bella before you captured my heart." She kissed him again. "No. You're not in this alone. I love you Daniel Callahan."

"By the way, thank you for saving me. That was so sweet of you." Nita kissed him, and he forgot about everything and everyone around him. She broke the kiss. "Stupid. But sweet." She kissed him again, this time slow and sensuous.

"I didn't really save you, you saved yourself." He held her tight in his arms and buried his face in the curve of her neck. "My kick-ass angel."

She glanced over her shoulder as the hallway filled with people. "I don't think we're a secret any longer."

"What are we going to do with him?" Lei Lu asked Katlin gesturing to the body on the floor.

Katlin didn't answer. She simply stared at Nita and Daniel, who completely ignored her and everyone else. "How did I miss that?"

EPILOGUE

"You shouldn't have brought all this food," Nita chastised Katlin as she lifted the plastic wrap off the top of a bowl of potato salad.

"You know me." Katlin tossed several ingredients into a fresh green salad. "I love to cook. My mother taught me never to come to a party empty-handed. Besides, other than MREs, can you cook real food?"

Nita smiled. "I'm learning." She looked around the large family kitchen of the home she'd shared with Daniel and the children for the past two weeks. Located in one of the Virginia suburbs of Washington D.C., the home itself was situated in what real estate agents call a reemerging neighborhood. The homes were older, but young couples were moving in and remodeling, bringing the houses up to modern designs and standards. After a life in apartments, Nita was going crazy filling all the space in the large home.

Katlin stopped and leaned against the granite countertop. "I've always liked this house. I think it's perfect for you and Daniel and the kids." Although this was not one of the houses she had inherited, Katlin did own it until a week ago when she deeded it to her brother. She had bought several homes in the D.C. area over the years and through the company she owned with her fiancé Alex Wolf. They rented them to the government as safe houses.

Nita had dreaded this conversation, but knew she had to have it now. "Are you sure you're okay with me and Daniel? Is it weird for you that we're together?"

Katlin threw her arms around Nita, and she instantly knew everything would be fine.

"I love you like a sister. After everything we've been through together, we're closer than siblings, especially if I use my relationship with Daniel as a yardstick." She released Nita and continued preparing the food. "To be honest with you, I didn't really know my brother while growing up. He was this much older boy who showed up every couple of months for a week or so, then he was gone again. For years, I didn't think he liked me. It wasn't until after Daddy died that I really got to know him. We were both adults by then and the only immediate family left for each other. Sure, we have Uncle Tom and Uncle Francis, but our parents are gone." Katlin gave Nita a one-armed hug. "You know exactly how that feels."

Nita's father had never been in her life. Her mother had been his long-term mistress, his dirty little secret who lived twenty miles away. He'd never forgotten Nita's birthday and generously provided for her at Christmas, but he'd also never been there for a single holiday. It had always been her and her mother. Ovarian cancer had taken her quickly Nita's junior year in undergraduate school. Fortunately, her ROTC scholarship and the insurance money had enabled her to finish her last two years before entering the Army.

She had wanted to go into cancer research when she started medical school, but an abandoned baby changed the direction of her life. Nita glanced toward the high chair and toddler seat at the dining room table, and realized another baby had changed her life again.

She took another bowl out of the refrigerator and began to remove the covering while Katlin laid lettuce, tomato, and onion on a large platter for the hamburgers. "So, you'd be okay with Daniel and me making this live-in arrangement more permanent?"

Katlin whirled around and grabbed her shoulders. "Do you think Daniel's going to ask you to marry him today?" Excitement was written all over the woman's face. "Is this really your engagement party, not a new home open house?"

"Oh, we wanted to have everyone over to see our new house, hang out on the deck, and swim in the pool," she reassured her friend.

The doorbell rang and Nita answered it. "Harper. Rafe. I'm so glad you were able to come."

Harper had gone through the Joint All-Female Special Operations School with all the Ladies of Black Swan. She and her fiancé, Rafe, lived two doors down from Katlin's condominium where all the Black Swans had suites.

"I hope you don't mind that I brought Marcus Hernandez with us." Harper silently begged with her eyes. "He's in town for additional ATF training for a few weeks and hanging out with us this weekend."

"No, no problem at all." Nita hugged each of the newcomers. "Marcus and I have gotten stupid drunk together more than once." She was suddenly glad she'd never slept with the tall, dark, and very handsome ATF agent. He'd always seemed attracted to Tori, although Nita wasn't sure if her friend even noticed.

"You promised we were never going to talk about Tori's birthday party again." Marcus grinned as he hugged her.

"Great house. Where do you want me to put these?" He held up a case of beer.

"There's a cooler on the deck. Everybody's out back." Nita gave them a brief tour as she led them through the house to the French doors.

When the doorbell rang again, she could hardly see the two men behind huge gift bags. "Uncle Tom, Monsignor Francis, it's great to see you."

"Where are the children?" Tom asked.

"Bella is napping and everyone else is out back. Perfect timing. We were just bringing the food out." Both men leaned over and gave her a kiss on the cheek.

"You look lovely, Nita." Uncle Tom gave her a warm smile. "It looks like you're ready for today."

She nervously giggled. "As ready as I'll ever be."

An hour later, Nita stretched out on a lounge chair and glanced around. Grace, Griffin, Katlin, and Alex were on one side of the water volleyball net and Tori, Marcus, Lei Lu, and Santiago were on the other side involved in a cutthroat game.

Cristobal Maximo, Uncle Tom, and Daniel took the chairs next to her.

"So, Cris, what happened after we left Central America?" Daniel poured more wine in Nita's glass and refilled his own.

"Last time I saw you two was in Managua." He smiled. "General Cortez showed up right after you left and told the former presidential guard they could either join his army or join their former president in jail."

"Exactly what is it you're doing here in the states, Cris?" Leave it to Uncle Tom to come straight to the point.

"General Cortez sent me here to show several congressional subcommittees exactly what the new Nicaraguan governmental plans include." Cris sipped his scotch. "We're going to need a lot of money to build the canal and railroad in the timeframe set out by your new president. The man is ambitious."

"Nicaragua needs that canal," Daniel stated. "It'll provide a future for the country's children for generations."

"You're preaching to the choir, my friend." Cris swirled the amber liquid in the crystal glass. "I just hope the United States keeps its promises."

The corners of Uncle Tom's mouth kicked up. "Ever since we gave back the Panama Canal, we've been looking for a fast, inexpensive way to move from the Atlantic to the Pacific. Don't be surprised if our government asks yours for a two-hundred-year contract."

Cris laughed openly. "Don't be surprised if my government says no." His face turned serious as he looked at Daniel. "Now that you're no longer in the spy business, or running guns for your government, would you consider being a lobbyist for the new Nicaraguan government?"

"Daniel already has a job," Uncle Tom interjected. "As soon as he's ready, he's going to be the lead Central American analyst."

Nita smiled. The job offer had come just the other day, and it would be perfect. Daniel would be permanently stationed in the United States, since technically his cover had been blown. His job would have regular hours Monday through Friday.

"So you have a desk job?" Without looking for confirmation, Cris turned toward Nita. "I take it you'll be sticking closer to home now? No more work with the CDC? Or was it the World Health Organization?"

"I'm actually active duty United States Army. Unfortunately, my job will continue to be unpredictable. I go wherever my government sends me." She sipped her wine.

Cris looked back and forth between Daniel and Nita. "Who will be taking care of my niece and nephew?"

Nita suddenly realized that Cris and Daniel would always be tied by the children.

"We hired an awesome nanny." Daniel had been so pleased when Katlin suggested Top Cooper's sister-in-law. She was perfect. Regrettably, she'd lost her husband a few months after she had retired from teaching first grade. With grown children, but no grandchildren yet, she was at a loss of how to stay busy. Simon and Bella would certainly fill her time.

A baby's stirring could be heard through the monitor next to Nita. Bella's nap was over and the next part of the day's activities were about to begin. "That's my signal. I need to go get baby Bella up and ready."

In a pretty white jumper with red flowers and bright green leaves, a miniature version of Nita's sundress, the two made an entrance on the deck.

Daniel, in his white and red Mexican guayabera shirt and khaki slacks walked over and kissed both of them. "You look beautiful. But that's not the only reason I love you." He took a deep breath and let it out slowly. He looked around and called, "Simon, out of the pool and get your shirt on."

Nita had to laugh. She didn't know who was more disappointed, Monsignor Francis or Simon.

Daniel put his arm around Nita as they waited for Simon to join them on the deck. "Nita and I want to thank you for joining us today," he announced. "Having all of you here has been absolutely wonderful. We want you all to feel welcome in our home. I suggest you call before dropping in, though." He gave Nita a quick kiss. "We might be busy."

That brought laughter from everyone.

"We also wanted all of you here for another reason." Daniel dropped to one knee.

All the women gasped. Except Nita.

"Nita Banks, you were my friend in the past, you are my friend in the present, and I want to ensure you are my friend in the future." He opened a ring box. Three round diamonds gleamed like droplets of water in the bright Virginian sun. "My father used to travel to Africa often, and he would buy my mother diamonds straight from the mine. Although she preferred blue diamonds, he often gave her white diamonds. He told me once the white diamond was like a woman, so many facets to the same gem, and all of them make her sparkle. I love every facet of you. You are the light in my life. Will you do me a great honor and agree to marry me, and brighten my life forever?"

Nita thought she'd been ready for this. Nothing could have prepared her for the beautiful words Daniel had said.

"Of course I'll marry you." Her throat had tightened, and she'd nearly choked on the words. He stood and slid the ring on her finger then kissed her—long, deep, and slow. Only when he withdrew did she realize everybody was whistling and clapping.

"So, when's the wedding?" Cris asked.

Daniel and Nita looked at each other, and then at Monsignor Francis Gilpatrick.

"Right now." Daniel picked up Simon and turned to face his uncle.

Surrounded by their friends and family, Nita and Daniel held their children as they pledged their lives to each other.

As soon as they had ended their first official kiss as husband and wife, Uncle Francis signaled for them to turn around. "Ladies and gentlemen, I'd like to present Mr. and Mrs. Daniel Callahan."

"You're now my mommy, right?" Simon asked amidst the clapping and cheers.

"Yes." A warmth like she'd never known filled her to overflowing. She was now mother to these two beautiful children whom she loved with all her heart. It was up to her and Daniel to raise them, protect them, and teach them. Daniel slid his arm around her and kissed her temple as though he knew her thoughts.

"Mommy," Simon called. "I gotta go potty."

Well, fu—...heck. She smiled at her official welcome to motherhood.

The End.

What's next for the Ladies of Black Swan?

Continue reading for a Sneak Peek at
Unbeatable Love: Marcus & Tori
Black Swan novel #5
Scarred outside and in, why would his beautiful friend ever want more with him?

UNBEATABLE LOVE

EXCERPT

No one was more surprised than Marcus Hernandez when his friend Katlin Callahan appeared in the window next to the driver of the semi and flashed a badge. When their gazes met she shook her head so slightly that if he hadn't been watching carefully he would have missed it. "This is going to take a while. Why don't you men get out and stretch your legs. Your load is secure. We have guards posted all the way around your rig."

Thank God for small favors. He couldn't wait to get out of the cab where he had been squeezed between two large men for over six hours without stopping. At just over six-feet, Marcus wasn't small, but he had the body of a long-distance runner rather than that of the linebackers who had sandwiched him in the truck. Ever since his...incident...and the subsequent surgeries, he found that muscles surrounding his once-broken bones tightened when he sat in one position too long. He'd passed that point hours ago.

As soon as all three men were on the ground, Katlin herded them to the side of the truck away from the prisoners. "Keep your face hidden," she ordered in a tone

Marcus had never heard from her before. It was brusque, and assertive. "I don't want anyone to be able to identify you."

Marcus slid a glance toward the line of approximately fifteen cuffed men and women. The guards were in all black, carrying military machine guns with more weapons strapped to their bodies. They looked and moved like the special operators he had worked with before. One by one they were handed off and escorted onto the black bus.

In the flashes of red, white, and blue emergency lights, he squinted to make out the tattoos on the men's faces and necks. Those were Salvadorian Vipers, SV-16, one of the fastest-growing gangs nationwide. Why had they been shooting at this truck? Had Katlin come from one of those cars that had protected them? He knew his friends worked for Homeland Security, and was aware they weren't your average female military officers, but he couldn't imagine why they were in the middle of Georgia on a nearly deserted interstate taking down gang members.

As he rounded the front of the cab, he could feel the heat pouring off the huge Peterbilt engine. One glance toward their precious cargo slapped him to reality. The SV-16 were trying to hijack their load of activated nuclear rods. In the wrong hands, the fissionable material in that trailer could give a terrorist gang more than enough firepower to flatten any major U.S. city.

Holy fuck.

"Stay here." Katlin stepped away speaking authoritatively into a hidden microphone.

Marcus had been on similar operations and knew she was probably speaking with some kind of a command center as well as everyone else involved. He looked at the other two men he'd just spent far too many hours cooped up with in a cab. Neither seemed to be connected to the op. When the driver's phone rang, he stepped aside.

Dash Lawson chuckled. "Looks like you and I are the only ones left out of this loop." The man from the Department of Energy was right.

Out of the corner of his eye, Marcus saw Katlin approach. "Agent Lawson, I'll brief you in a minute. Agent Hernandez, follow me."

Katlin led the way to the very end of the trailer. He recognized Grace Hall as she stood guard, rifle to her shoulder scoping the area between the gravel road side and the tree line fifty feet away. He didn't say anything to her. He knew better.

"Hey, Marcus. Thanks for holding our cover. If you need to call to me, my handle is Lady Hawk." Katlin constantly scanned her surroundings, keeping a close eye on the prisoners and their guards. She held the machine gun so casually, as though she did it every day. "For now, don't speak to anyone other than me. If I'm not able to explain everything by the end of this op, I promise you I'll tell you what I can when we get home."

Home. Although they didn't live in the same building, he spent lots of time on the top floor of the DuPont Circle condo where Katlin and her team lived. He hung out with his former ATF team member, Harper Tambini, and her fiancé Rafe Silva, who worked for Katlin's fiancé, Alex Wolf. Sometimes Washington D.C. was really a small place.

"Will do, Lady Hawk." He gave her his crooked smile. It was the best he could manage, but she understood. Many of the muscles in his face still didn't work correctly, even after four surgeries. At least they had been able to repair the muscles around his mouth when they restructured his broken jaw, and after nearly a year of speech therapy, he could form almost every word properly. They were still working on matching both sides of his face and reducing the jagged scar that started at the corner of his eye and crossed his cheek. He was able to hide part of the thick red line under his beard that also covered several of the surgical scars. Maybe someday he wouldn't look like Frankenstein's monster.

Since his incident nearly two years ago, he hadn't found many women who could see beyond his disfigured face long enough to get naked with him. Of the few he had managed to get into bed, they fell into two categories. There were the women who were curious and wanted to examine every scar as closely as his dermatologist. These women wanted to hear all the gory details of how he had been captured in the United States by a Colombian cartel and beaten within a breath of his life. The other women he had convinced to have sex with him, didn't want to touch him. They were appalled, not in pity for him and what he had endured for nearly two days, but for themselves for having to see such damaged skin. One woman had even demanded he keep his T-shirt on as they had sex. If he hadn't been so aroused, he would have walked away. Needless to say, he never dated any of those women again.

Katlin's attention was diverted by something she obviously heard in her ear. She mouthed the word *sorry* then headed toward the bus where one of the women was refusing to enter. Marcus watched her determined strides. She was one of the six women who didn't seem to notice his physical impairments. All of them were physically gorgeous women, but good down to the bone. They were truly his friends.

After one of his operations, he hadn't wanted to return to the lonely postsurgical rehabilitation center, so Harper offered to take care of him at her place since Rafe was in training in Miami. When she had been called out on an explosives job in

Oregon, Katlin and her friends moved him to their apartment next door and took care of him. They were like the sisters he never had. With one exception.

His mind immediately went to Tori. What he felt for the beautiful, former model, was far from sisterly. Even before the cartel had beat the shit out of him, he'd known she was way out of his league. Hell, he had no idea how to even play that game. He wasn't good enough back then for the most stunning woman he'd ever met, and now, he was thrilled when the lovely woman merely glanced his way. Relegated to the friend zone, the only way she'd go out with him was because she'd pitied him and he couldn't handle that, especially from her.

Out of the darkness, a tall feminine figure strode toward him. He'd know that walk anywhere. He had memorized the distinct curves of her lithe body. The gentle sway of her hips as she placed one foot almost exactly in front of the other, eating up the distance between them with a stride nearly as long as his own. Damn, the woman had the most attractive long legs, currently hid underneath baggie black cargo pants tucked into military boots.

"Hi, Marcus," Tori said with a smile when she was five feet away. "I didn't expect to see you out here in bumfuck Georgia in the middle of the night." She glanced up at the semi. "I take it you're here in an official capacity?"

He gave her his half-grin because he couldn't see her and not smile. "Yeah. ATF had reliable intelligence that someone was targeting the nuclear shipments." He chuckled. "I guess they were right." His gaze trailed off toward the bus as the last of the terrorists were being loaded. "But as usual, we were behind the power curve. I was along for the ride to see what security measures were in place and to suggest enhancements."

For a long second he studied her perfect face. Dark skin, far from black, closer to the color of a cream-rich latte, he wondered about her heritage. When they had started to rebuild his face, they asked him if he wanted to change his appearance, and if so, what nationality he preferred. Since then, he had spent hours studying facial features.

She had high cheekbones like those of Native Americans, yet her eyes were very large and oval in shape. Her nose was slightly squatty as though she had some African mixed in but her flawlessly bowed lips spoke of northern Europeans. He supposed she was a conglomeration, like most Americans. Being the melting pot, she was likely to have a little bit of everything in her genealogy. However, the Greek goddess Aphrodite must have blessed her with the gift of beauty. As Tori stood regally in front of him, almost at eye level, he couldn't believe she was actually talking to him. Yes. It was work related. He touched his most recent scar next to the outside of his left eye where they were rebuilding the socket.

Refocusing on their surroundings, he asked, "So, is this what your team does? Security for the Department of Energy? Protecting loads of uranium?"

Her sideways glance and hesitation gave him his answer.

Tori returned her gaze to him. "That's what we did tonight." She gave him a halfhearted smile. "We're all still active duty military. We do whatever the hell they tell us to do."

"But you're still with Homeland Security, right?" Marcus stared as the last prisoner was loaded onto the bus. "I guess I can see how SV-16 could be considered a terrorist group, or are you working with immigration?"

Tori burst out laughing. "I'm the last person who knows who the fuck I'm working for tonight. They just tell us where to go, who to meet, and what's our goal." She threw her hands in the air. "Tonight, this was it. Tomorrow night we could be wearing ball gowns and dancing with congressional staffers at a state dinner."

Marcus knew how stunning Tori was in a full-length gown. When he was homebound in Katlin's condo, Tori had been assigned a job at a White House function. Sore, aching, and drugged with postsurgical painkillers, he still managed to get hard when she had walked into the condo asking for someone to zip up the dress. Lounging on the couch, most of his face wrapped in bandages, he was thankful for his one good eye. He touched the softest skin as he pulled up the zipper, dodging sequins. She'd smelled like heaven. All he'd wanted to do was brush his lips over every inch of skin exposed by the low back.

Jokingly, Marcus wiggled his fingers. "If you need help getting into, or out of a dress, I'm more than happy to help."

She held his gaze as a slow sensual smile crossed her face. "That can be dangerous."

"Yes, it could." Marcus had been good at flirting... before...but he knew what he looked like now. He hadn't been movie star handsome, but he'd had a Latin lover look about him that seemed to attract women. The fact that he loved to dance, especially in the salsa style he'd grown up with, never hurt his chances in leaving a nightclub with a woman.

But all that was in his past. He still faced several more surgeries, each with the caveat that they would do their best but there were no guarantees.

He stepped back into the shadows so Tori didn't have to see his face.

"Do you have to go?" Tori tilted her head to where the driver and Dash stood talking quietly.

He should go before things got awkward between the two

of them. Not that he liked the friend zone, but he knew she was comfortable with him in that box.

Nodding, he said, "Yeah. I should get back to them."

"You're unarmed." Tori tilted her head toward her rifle. "I'll walk you back."

He wasn't about to argue if it meant spending even a few more seconds with her.

Tori touched her ear then said quietly, "I'm escorting ATF Special Agent Marcus Hernandez back to the driver."

As they approached the other two men, Dash's phone rang. He didn't bother stepping away. "Lawson." There was a long silence while the Department of Energy agent simply listened. "You're fucking with me?" He closed his eyes and tilted his face toward the starless night. "Who knows about this?" Dash dropped his head and held Tori's gaze. "I'll handle informing the other agencies."

Thumbing the off button, Dash glanced between Tori and Marcus. "You're not fucking going to believe this." His arm shot out, finger-pointing at the trailer. "This was a decoy. There are no nuclear weapons in that trailer. Some fucking genius in the Transportation Department decided to send out two loads tonight. We got the decoy. The real rods were only twenty miles from the Navy base when they were hijacked." He rolled in his lips and glanced away.

After a few deep breaths, Dash seemed to have his emotions under control. "The driver and..." He cleared his throat. "Both the driver and the DOE agent were found dead in the truck. The trailer is gone." He looked at Marcus. "And so is the nuclear material."

"How accurate is your source?" Tori took a step toward Dash, fury in her large brown eyes.

"Completely." Daschle swallowed hard. "When the driver didn't report in within five minutes of his ETA, protocol is to make contact. When nobody answered their phones, transportation has to contact the state police. My boss is on the scene."

"General Lyon, we have a situation." Tori's report was brief and accurate. The roar on the other end of the line forced her to pull her communications unit out of her ear. She glared at Daschle. "I don't know how to break this to you, but USSOCOM doesn't like to be lied to. The idiot who made that decision won't have a job tomorrow." She screwed the earpiece back in.

She started walking away but after two steps spun around and got into Daschle's face. "I need you to open the back of that trailer. I have been ordered by the President of the United States to verify that there are no nuclear materials in that trailer." She poked his chest. "I'm sure you have a portable Geiger counter somewhere in that truck. Get it."

Twenty minutes later, both Tori and Katlin had walked up and down the aisle between the boxes verifying the lack of fissionable materials. Their cargo was new, unarmed missiles to be loaded onto a submarine and armed with the nuclear rods on the other truck.

"General Lyon is pissed." Katlin wasn't telling the group anything they didn't already know.

Marcus glanced around the makeshift circle taking in the reactions. The eight men in black reacted as though the situation was nothing new for them. All five of his female friends looked disgusted.

"What a fucking waste of time." Nita shook her head.

Marcus hadn't considered it a complete waste. He learned several things about the women he'd known for over a year, including their codenames or handles. Nita Banks Callahan, who had recently married Katlin's brother, Daniel, and gained a little boy and an infant girl in the process, went by Lady

Harrier when on an op. The newly engaged Grace Hall was Lady Eagle, Lei Lu Sorensen was Lady Kite, and Tori's code name was Lady Falcon. She looked like the bird of prey with her talons extended, anger seething beneath the well-controlled emotions.

All at once, everyone else started moving. The quiet men in black headed toward the vehicles they'd arrived in after mumbling quietly, obviously talking to someone in their headsets. Daschle's phone rang and after looking at the caller ID, he stepped aside. The driver's phone rang a second later and he wandered around his truck as though inspecting its condition.

All five women surrounded Marcus with smiles, tapping something next to their ears, probably turning off audio. The conversation was going to be private.

"Thanks for handling this well and not giving away that you know us." Katlin looked at the retreating backs of the special operators. "We try to keep our private lives just that, private." She let out a heavy breath. "Now that we cleared that up, we've been ordered to leave. We'll see you back in D.C."

With goodbyes and thank-yous from the other women, they all turned and walked away...except Tori. She stepped closer.

"We haven't seen you in weeks." Her voice was filled with concern. She touched his bicep and gave it a light squeeze. "Don't be such a stranger. You know you're welcome anytime. You have my number. Call. Text. Let me know how you're doing. Please." She squeezed his upper arm a little harder and held it longer before releasing her grasp and walking away.

He hadn't missed the change from *we* to *me*. Marcus smiled as he touched his arm where the heat from her body was already cooling. Did she really want him to call her? Just her? Was she worried about his physical condition? Or maybe even about his mental state? Or did Tori want him to call her so they could talk?

The vibration of his ringing phone in his pocket startled him out of thoughts. Looked like his next orders were coming through.

He hesitated as the luscious female form of Tori Denton disappeared into the darkness.

"Hernandez."

This concludes your Sneak Peek at
Unbeatable Love: Marcus & Tori
Black Swan Novel #5
Available in all formats
https://kalyncooper.com/unbeatable-love

BOOKS BY KALYN COOPER

If you've enjoyed *Unguarded Love,* please tell others what you liked about this book by leaving a review on your retailer's site.

You may also wish to consider other books by KaLyn Cooper...

Black Swan Series
Military active duty women secretly trained in Special Operations and the men who dare to capture the heart of a Woman Warrior.

Unconventional Beginnings Prequel (Black Swan novella #0.5) ~ He's dead. But they can't allow it to affect her. She's too important.
Download FREE https://dl.bookfunnel.com/uec4utb66d

Unrelenting Love: Lady Hawk (Katlin) & Alex (Black Swan novel #1) ~ Women in special operations? Never... Until he sleeps with the most lethal woman in the world.

Noel's Puppy Power: Bailey & Tanner (A Sweet Christmas Black Swan novella #1.5) ~ He's better at communicating with animals than women, but as an amputee she knows firsthand it's the internal scars that can be most difficult to heal.

Uncaged Love: Harper & Rafe (Black Swan novel #2) ~ The jungle isn't the only thing that's hot while escaping from a Colombian cartel.

Unexpected Love: Lady Eagle (Grace) & Griffin (Black Swan novel #3) ~ He never believed in love, but he never expected to find her.

Challenging Love: Katlin & Alex (A Black Swan novella #3.5) ~ A new relationship can be fragile when outsiders are determined to challenge that love.

Unguarded Love: Lady Harrier (Nita) & Daniel (Black Swan novel #4) ~ She couldn't lose another sick baby...then he brought her his dying daughter.

Choosing Love: Grace & Griffin (A Black Swan novella #4.5) ~ Hard choices have to be made when parents interfere in a growing relationship.

Unbeatable Love: Lady Falcon (Tori) & Marcus (Black Swan novel #5) ~ Scarred outside and in, why would his beautiful friend ever want more with him?

Unmatched Love: Lady Kite (Lei Lu) & Henry (Black Swan novel #6) ~ Scarred outside and in, why would his beautiful friend ever want more with him?

Unending Love: Lady Falcon (Tori) & Marcus (Black Swan novel #7) ~ Their life together is not over. He has to believe it...or it will be.

Guardian Elite Series
Former special operators, these men work for Guardian Security (from the Black Swan Series) protecting families in their homes and executives on the road, but they can't always protect their hearts.

Double Jeopardy (Novella #1 Guardian Elite series crossover with Hildie McQueen's Indulgences series) ~ Guarding a billionaire and his wife isn't easy when you can't keep your eyes off your bikini wearing, gun carrying partner who is lethal in stilettos.

Justice for Gwen (Novella #2 Guardian Elite series crossover with Susan Stoker's Special Forces World) ~ She's not what she seems. Neither is he. But the terrorist threat is real. So is the desire that smolders between them.

Rescuing Melina (Novella #3 Guardian Elite series crossover with Susan Stoker's Special Forces World) ~ When Jacin awoke stateside, he remembered nothing about his escape from the Colombian cartel or his torture. He was sure of only one thing, his love of Melina, his handler. When she disappears, neither bruises nor the CIA will keep him from rescuing her.

Snow SEAL (Novella #4 Guardian Elite series crossover with Elle James Brotherhood Protectors World) ~ Terrorists want her...but so does he. The chase isn't the only thing that heats up when the flint of the former SEAL strikes against the steel of the woman warrior.

Securing Willow (Novella #5 Guardian Elite series crossover with Susan Stoker's Special Forces World) ~ Guarding her wasn't his job, but he couldn't let her die...even before she stole his heart. When he discovers the temptingly beautiful foreign service officer is being threatened, his protective instincts take over.

SEAL in a Storm (Novel #5 is part of the Suspense Sisters new wave of connected books, Silver SEALs featuring a seasoned hero and heroine, second chances, and edge of your seat suspense.) ~ With a hurricane bearing down on the tiny island, they only have days to find and rescue ten kidnapped young girls and their chaperones...and keep their hands off each other.

Cancun Series

Follow the Girard family —along with their friends, former SEALs and active duty female Navy pilots—as they hunt Mayan antiquities, terrorists and Mexican cartels in what most would call paradise. Tropical nights aren't the only thing HOT in Cancun.

Christmas in Cancun (Cancun Series Book #1) ~ Can the former SEAL keep his libido in check and his family safe when the quest for ancient Mayan idols turns murderous?

Conquered in Cancun (Cancun Series Novella #1.5) ~ A helicopter pilot's second chance at love walks into a Cancun nightclub, but she's a jet fighter pilot with reinforced walls around her heart.

Captivated in Cancun (Cancun Series Book #2) ~ His job is tracking down terrorists so he's not interested in a family. She wants him short-term, then needs him when their worlds collide.

Claimed by a SEAL (Cancun Series crossover Novella #2.5 with Cat Johnson's Hot SEALs) ~ How far will the Homeland Security agent go to assure mission success when forced undercover for a second time with an irresistible SEAL?

Never Series

The mission brought the five of them together, disaster nearly tore them apart, a mystery and killer reunited them forever.

A Love Never Forgotten (Never Series novel #1) ~ Dreams or nightmares. Truth or lies. He can't tell them apart. Then he discovers the woman who has haunted his dreams is real. Is she his future? Or his past?

A Promise Never Forgotten (Never Series novel #2) ~ As a Marine Lieutenant Colonel, he could take on any mission and succeed. Raising his two godchildren…with her…just might kill him.

A Moment Never Forgotten (Never Series novel #3) ~ The moment he realized she was in serious danger…he couldn't protect her.

ABOUT THE AUTHOR

KaLyn Cooper is a USA Today Bestselling author whose romances blend fact and fiction with blazing heat and heart-pounding suspense. Life as a military wife has shown KaLyn the world, and thirty years in PR taught her that fact can be stranger than fiction. She leaves it up to the reader to separate truth from imagination. She, her husband, and Little Bear (Alaskan Malamute) live in Tennessee on a micro-plantation filled with gardens, cattle, and quail. When she's not writing, she's at the shooting range or paddling on the river.

For the latest on works in progress and future releases, check out
KaLyn Cooper's website www.KaLynCooper.com
http://www.kalyncooper.com/

Follow **KaLyn Cooper on Facebook** for promotions and giveaways
https://www.facebook.com/KaLynCooper1Author/

Sign up for exclusive promotions and special offers only available in **KaLyn's newsletter** https://kalyncooper.com/kalyn-cooper-newsletter